English translation of novel Namaste which has been originally published in Hindi Language

NAMASTE

Manu Saunkhala

Rajmangal Prakashan

An Imprint of **Rajmangal Publishers**

ISBN : 978-8119251100

Published by :

Rajmangal Publishers

Rajmangal Prakashan Building,
Ozone, Quarsi, Ramghat Road
Aligarh-202001, (UP) INDIA
Cont. No. +91- 7017993445
www.rajmangalpublishers.com
rajmangalpublishers@gmail.com
sampadak@rajmangalpublishers.in

प्रथम संस्करण : जुलाई 2022 – पेपरबैक

प्रकाशक : राजमंगल प्रकाशन

राजमंगल प्रकाशन बिल्डिंग,

ओजोन, क्वार्सी, रामघाट रोड,

अलीगढ़, उप्र. – 202001, भारत

फ़ोन : +91 - 7017993445

First Published : July 2023 - Paperback
Printed by : Thomson Press India Ltd, Repro India Ltd & Manipal Tech Ltd.
eBook by : Rajmangal ePublishers (Digital Publishing Division)

Cover design: Girish Malap

Table Of Contents

1: The Mysteries of the Universe any cycles of Life on Earth

The universe has always been shrouded in mystery, and the curiosity about its origin continues to baffle humankind. It's been billions of years since the universe came into being, yet we still don't have a clear understanding of how it all began. We know that the universe is made up of various elements, but why was it created? When did it all start? And how long will it last? These are questions that have eluded us for eons.

It is believed by the majority that; the universe was born from a massive explosion that occurred billions of years before. This explosion set off a chain reaction, creating countless constellations, planets and satellites that together make up what we know as the universe and with this explosion, time itself began.

Time is a mysterious concept, and it differs from planet to planet and satellite to satellite for an observer. There is a mysterious force that drives the universe forward. The energy that created the universe is the same energy that flows through every living being in the cosmos, regardless of its form.

The stars that make up the constellations are the source of light and energy in the universe. The planets that revolve around these stars are home to countless life forms.

Far, far away from the heart of the universe lies a wondrous star, known as the Sun. It is the center of a remarkable solar system, which is home to nine unique planets, each of them dancing around the Sun in perfect harmony. And nestled within this system is a single, awe-inspiring planet called Earth, which teems with life in all its magnificent forms - from soaring birds and majestic trees, to all manner of animals and the most remarkable of them all, humans. Human beings are the crown jewel of Earth's natural wonders, and their curious minds and boundless potential make them the most remarkable creatures in this enigmatic world. Earth is the most unique, as it is the only one that sustains human life.

Every living being on Earth is made up of the five fundamental elements which give it physical form. However, there are other elements that are not visible to the naked eye, and these elements bind every living being to the cycle of karma. These elements include ego, love, greed attachment, fear, lust, jealousy, desire, austerity, and anger. It is only humans who have the power to understand the effects of these invisible elements, and it is through their supreme knowledge that they can conquer them.

Throughout history, God has taken human incarnation time and again to impart this ultimate knowledge to humanity. It is only through this knowledge that we can unravel the secrets of creation and understand the purpose of our existence.

The cycle of life on Earth is divided into four parts: *Satyuga, Tretayuga, Dwaparyuga, and Kaliyuga.* During *Satyuga*, truth and selfless love were the dominant virtues, and every creature on Earth lived together in harmony. In *Tretayuga*, however, falsehood, hatred, lust, and greed began to increase due to the ignorance of the Asuras. God incarnated during this time to vanquish the Asuras and saved the creatures of the Earth.

During *Dwaparyuga*, there was a great war between dharma and adharma, and it was only through God 's intervention that dharma emerged victorious.

With the end of *Dwaparyuga*, a dark period of time known as *Kaliyuga* descends upon the earth, foretelling chaos and destruction. This tumultuous era marks the final chapter in the four-part cycle of life on earth. And when the end finally arrives, it brings with it a catastrophic *Mahapralay* submersing every visible matter, heralding the beginning of a new life form and a fresh start for the world.

2. *Mahabharata: A Tale of Power Struggles and Moral Dilemmas*

Bharatvarsh, a land encompassed by the mighty Himalayan ranges and the vast ocean, has been the epicenter of power for thousands of years for the entire earth. It is not just a land but a beacon of knowledge for humanity across the globe. This tale unfurls an unparalleled saga of power struggles in Bharatvarsh, set in the transition from Dwaparyuga to Kaliyuga, commencing with the legendary battle of Mahabharata at Kurukshetra.

As one journeys past the high peaks of the Himalayas and traverses many valleys, the place named Kurukshetra come into view. The sky is shrouded in a thick blanket of clouds, casting a dim light over the battlefield below. Two massive armies stand poised for battle, with the Kauravas of the Kuru dynasty facing off against the Pandavas. Warriors from all corners of the world have assembled on this hallowed ground, with Bhishma Pitamah, Guru Drona, Mahavir Karna, and Duryodhana leading the charge for the Kauravas, and Yudhishthira, Bhima, and Arjuna marshaling their troops for the Pandavas.

Each warrior is armed with his deadliest weapons, and millions of soldiers stand ready to face each other in a fierce battle. Even though everyone tried to stop the war, no one could come to peaceful decisions. When dialogues and diplomacy failed, the path of war was chosen. Now, whoever wins this war, their virtues will be remembered in history close to the truth.

Amidst the chaos and carnage, Prabhu Shri Krishna himself has chosen to participate in the war as the charioteer of Arjuna. His curly hair cascades down his broad shoulders, his muscular frame exuding a sense of strength and power. His charming smile can disarm even his deadliest foes, making them his friends. The presence of Prabhu Shri Krishna with the Pandavas has already ensured their victory in this war, but Bhishma Pitamah, Guru Drona, and Mahavir Karna, all wise warriors of the Kauravas, know that the Pandavas cannot be defeated with Prabhu Shri Krishna on their side. Despite this knowledge, all the warriors are committed to fulfilling their vows, their commitments, and their friendships, standing resolutely on the battlefield, ready to face whatever fate has in store for them.

As the war loomed ahead, Arjuna found himself torn seeing his own kin among the ranks of his foes. The whole of Bharatvarsh knew that Bhishma Pitamah held Arjuna in the highest regard, yet here he was, ready to fight and defeat him. Guru Drona, who had always favored Arjuna and even asked Eklavya for his right thumb to ensure that he does not become better than Arjuna. The very thought of killing his own relatives made Arjuna tremble with fear, tears streaming down his face as he laid down his beloved Gandiva bow. He no longer wished to fight this war.

Turning to Prabhu Shri Krishna, Arjuna pleaded, "Oh, Shri Krishna! I see no good in killing my own kin or gaining the kingdom by doing so. Even if I were to be granted all three Lokas, I would not fight against them."

Then seeing Arjuna with eyes filled with compassion, mourning, tears, Shri Krishna said - O Arjuna! Where did this ignorance come from in your mind? This ignorance is not at all favorable for a human being who knows the value of life, it does not lead to higher lokas but infamy. It doesn't suit you. Abandon the weakness of your heart and stand up for war.

"How am I supposed to shoot my arrows at revered figures like Pitamah Bhishma and Guru Drona?" Arjuna asked. "I would rather beg for my sustenance than take the lives of these noble souls. Even if they are motivated by worldly desires, they are still my teachers. If I were to slay them, every morsel I ate would be tainted with their blood. I am torn between two paths: to conquer them, or to be conquered by them. I do not know which fate is better for me."

Arjuna's voice trembled as he spoke, his hands folded in front of him. "I have forgotten my duty," he confessed. "I am now your disciple and seek your guidance. Please, guide me. I cannot see any path that will relieve me of this overwhelming sorrow."

Arjuna looked to Vasudev (*Prabhu Shri Krishna*), his eyes pleading for answers. "I cannot bring myself to fight," he continued, his voice growing quieter. With a heavy heart, he fell silent.

Prabhu Shri Krishna's smile remained as he addressed Arjuna once again. "O Arjuna!" he said. "You grieve for those who are not worthy of your sorrow. The wise do not mourn for the living or the dead."

Krishna's voice held a deep sense of knowing as he continued. " It has never happened that I have not been there, or you have not been there, or all these kings have not been there. Just as the soul progresses through childhood, youth, and old age within the same body, so too does it move on to another body after death. The wise do not become captivated by such changes."

Krishna's eyes shone with brilliant light as he spoke of the soul. "The physical body is not permanent, but the soul remains unchanged. No one can destroy the soul. It neither takes birth nor dies, and it is never killed, even when the body perishes. The person who knows the soul is imperishable and eternal, how can he kill or be killed? Just as a person discards old clothes and dons new ones, the soul discards old bodies and takes on new ones."

Krishna's tone shifted to one of urgency as he spoke of duty. "Death is inevitable for those who are born, and rebirth after death is certain. You must not neglect your duty and incur sin. If you do not fight, you will lose your reputation as a warrior. Infamy is worse than death for a respected person."

He turned to Arjuna with final advice. "O Arjuna! Fight without concern for happiness or sorrow, loss or gain, victory or defeat."

Prabhu Shri Krishna bequeathed the ultimate knowledge to humanity through Arjuna. The sage Ved Vyas chronicled the knowledge for posterity. Prabhu Shri Krishna foresaw that the Kaliyuga, an age of darkness, was imminent. He intended for the knowledge to serve as a guiding light for future generations, helping them stay on the righteous path and not succumb to the perils of Kaliyuga.

Empowered by Prabhu Krishna's teachings, Arjuna rose to battle against the Kauravas in Kurukshetra. The ferocious battle was ultimately won by the Pandavas, thanks to Prabhu Shri Krishna's guidance. Yudhishthira was crowned the King of Bharatvarsh after the war. However soon after the war, Prabhu Shri Krishna eventually left his human form and returned to his divine abode, leaving Pandavas heartbroken and detached from the world. They entrusted the kingdom's reins to Parikshit and embarked on a journey to the Himalayas. Thus, after their departure, Arjuna's grandson and Abhimanyu's son, Parikshit, ascended the throne of Bharatvarsh.

3. The Rise of Kaliyuga: The Beginning of the End

As Prabhu Shri Krishna departed from the mortal world, the era of Dwaparyuga came to an end, and the era of Kaliyuga began. Manvantar Loka, a world situated 100 light years away from earth, brimmed with energy but remained strangely cool. This massive loka floated in the sky, shining like a beam of light and revolving around the center of the universe. The Kaliyuga, dormant for eons, has stirred from its slumber and begun its ominous march towards the Manvantar Loka. Beware, for the very nature of Kaliyuga is to bring about destruction. It does not know the extent of its own malevolence. Its awakening is a harbinger of our planet life hurtling towards its ultimate demise, where we, the human race, shall be the architects of our own destruction through our actions, and the role of Kaliyuga will be the deciding factor. Kaliyuga arrived at Manvantar Loka with the speed of light. Dwapar was reluctant to depart but had no choice but to yield to the arrival of Kaliyuga.

Kaliyuga appeared before Dwapar, dressed in black, youthful and vibrant. The sunlight sparkled from his earrings, and his shoulder-length hair was a flowing mane of darkness. His long teeth and nose portrayed his malevolence. On the other hand, Dwapar had aged, his hair had turned white, and his brilliance had faded, unable to withstand the strong effects of Kaliyuga.

Manvantar Loka, distinct from any constellation or planet, thrived on the deeds of humanity. At that time, Earth was the only planet in the solar system with life, and the actions of humans on earth were the only source of energy for Manvantar Loka.

As Kaliyuga gazed upon the beauty of this grand loka, he smiled and spoke to Dwapar. "Your time in Manvantar Loka is over, and now the solar system shall function according to my will. I will determine the nature of the humans on earth."

Dwapar said while being distressed - O Kaliyuga! Your rise is meant for destruction. But don't consider humans so weak. Humans are wise. They will not become your slaves just by your wish.

Kaliyuga laughed heartily, dismissing Dwapar's concerns. "Ha! Humans are nothing but weaklings. They shall bow down to me and do my bidding, serving my every whim. Their actions shall serve to empower me."

As Dwapar stared at Kaliyuga, he knew that his words would fall on deaf ears. Together, they arrived at the court of Manvantar Loka where the very virtues and vices that governed the universe were present in human form. In this court, Austerity, Compassion, and Love represented the virtues and wore white while Anger, Greed, Attachment, and Lust represented the vices and donned black. These virtue and vices resided within every human and gained strength or weakness depending on their actions. During Dwapar's era, these vices were controlled and weakened, but Kaliyuga sought to unleash them as his assistants. As a result, Austerity, Compassion, and Love began to wither, and all were forced to submit to Kaliyuga's court. Dwapar watched with a heavy heart, unable to stop the inevitable due to the laws of the universe.

As his time drew to a close, Dwapar made his way towards the final gate of Manvantar Loka where he looked at Kaliyuga one last time. He gazed into his eyes and spoke his final words, "Love the human beings for whom you are the governor of Manvantar Loka." With a bright light enveloping him, Dwapar merged into the universe, completing his cycle.

Kaliyuga sat atop the throne, radiating with delight at his newfound power. His court of seven entities stood in awe of him, with anger being the first to pay his respects. "Welcome, Swami! We are thrilled to have you here. As you know, Earth is the source of energy for Manvantar Loka, and we must make humans work for us to regain our strength," he said with reverence.

Kaliyuga laughed, "Undoubtedly! We will only be empowered when we control human karma."

Lust joined in, "Lord, you have freed us from Dwaparyuga's limitations. We are stronger now."

Now Kaliyuga's gaze wandered over the earth, settling on the land where Prabhu Shri Krishna was born. After observing it for a moment, he spoke gravely, "Parikshit, ruler of Bharatvarsh, is a formidable obstacle. As long as he reigns, we cannot control humans on Earth. We must put an end to his rule."

Anger leaped with enthusiasm, "Swami, I am at full strength thanks to your arrival. I can complete this task without fail. Just give me the order!"

Kaliyuga chuckled, "Make sure King Parikshit falls under your control. Your power over human behavior is fleeting, for in those moments, they are capable of bringing about their own downfall."

In the court of Kaliyuga, the vices of Greed, Attachment, and Lust eagerly awaited their chance to serve their new master. However, Kaliyuga chose Anger to carry out his plan.

Kaliyuga looked around the court and addressed everyone present, "Every entity has its time and place, and at this moment, Anger is the most effective tool to achieve our goals." Turning to the Austerity, Compassion and Love Kaliyuga declared that their golden age had ended with Prabhu Shri Krishna's departure, and they would now be his slaves. But Austerity spoke up and defended the humans' wisdom, only to be met with laughter from Kaliyuga and his cohorts.

With his mind set on bringing Parikshit to his knees, Kaliyuga sent anger to Earth. Parikshit's rule stood in the way of Kaliyuga's victory over humanity, and with Anger's help, he would soon be dethroned.

4. The Reign of Rajan Parikshit

Bharatvarsh, the land of wealth and knowledge, sprawls over most of the Earth's land. The snow-capped Himalayas, the crown of this land, are the origin of all the rivers. These rivers flow through the plains and merge into the ocean, irrigating the lands they pass by.

More than half of the land of Bharatvarsh is covered in dense forests, where many wild animals roam free, living by the rules of nature without any fear. Humans act as custodians of nature in this land. The capital of Bharatvarsh is Hastinapur, a vast city located in the north of the country, where King Parikshit rules with his able governance.

Parikshit ascended to the throne at a young age after the Pandavas had gone to the Himalayas. However, he was no less than his ancestors in terms of his abilities and strength. He was the son of the valiant Abhimanyu and the grandson of Arjuna, the greatest warrior of his time. Parikshit learned the art of governance from Dharmraj Yudhishthira, and he was a people-loving king who never let the nation feel the absence of Dharmraj Yudhishthira during his reign. He always fulfilled his duties towards his people with great dedication and welfare.

As long as Parikshit ruled Bharatvarsh, it was impossible for Kaliyuga to enslave humans. The king's wisdom and strength were a great obstacle for the forces of evil that threatened to invade his kingdom.

Kaliyuga's plot to destroy King Parikshit had set anger on his trail. For days, the furious emotion chased the king like a tempest, but Parikshit's intellect remained steadfast and refused to let anger consume him. The frustration of anger grew as it failed to gain the upper hand over the wise king.

One fateful day, Parikshit ventured into the forest with his officers to hunt wild deer. But a twist of fate caused them to lose their way, and the king found himself alone and lost amidst the thorny bushes. His once royal clothes were now torn, and the intense heat left him in a pitiable state. He experienced a level of discomfort he had never felt before.

After wandering through the dense forest for what felt like hours, Parikshit's eyes finally fell upon an ashram, nestled amidst the trees. Anger had been waiting for months, waiting for the right moment to strike, and finally, it found him.

As he entered the ashram, Parikshit's thirst and weariness overwhelmed him, and he sought water from a sage who appeared to be deep in meditation in that ashram. However, despite his plea, the sage remained lost in his trance, oblivious to Parikshit's needs.

Anger took hold of Parikshit at that moment. His frustration at being ignored by the sage ignited a flame of rage within him. In an impulsive fit of anger, he picked a dead snake with his arrow, lying nearby and flung it around the sage's neck before storming out of the ashram.

As King Parikshit stormed out of the ashram, he caught sight of his soldiers waiting for him a short distance away. They quickly offered him water, and he made his way back to the palace. However, the anger that had possessed him lingered on at the ashram where he had acted out in rage against sage whose name was Shamik.

Moments later, Shringi, the son of the disgraced sage, arrived at the ashram and was outraged to see his father's mistreatment. At this moment, Anger overpowered his intellect, and he cursed whoever was responsible for the heinous act. "Whoever has done this act," he seethed, "that person will die of snakebite after seven days from today."

King Parikshit had finally returned to his palace, but the guilt of his actions weighed heavily on his heart. As he stepped into his chamber, he could feel the flames of repentance burning within him. He was consumed by his own shame, and even the presence of his ministers failed to console him. Parikshit was the descendant of Arjuna, the great warrior who led the Pandavas to victory in the epic battle of Mahabharata. His own father, Abhimanyu, was a hero whose bravery was still celebrated throughout Bharatvarsh. And yet, Parikshit had acted in a way that would have made them both ashamed of him. He was no longer fit to be called the successor of Dharmraj Yudhishthira. These thoughts now spilled out of his eyes in the form of tears, as he realized the magnitude of his wrongdoing.

As sage Shamik emerged from his penance, he sensed something was amiss. His disciples, including his son Shringi, were in the ashram. The wise sage was deeply upset upon hearing what had transpired. He turned to his son and admonished him, saying that he has made a grave mistake by cursing King Parikshit without considering the consequences. Parikshit is a man of great honor, who follows the teachings of the Shastras. The punishment of death was far too severe for his transgressions. The sage realized the gravity of the situation and sent a person to warn the king in the Raj Bhavan so that he could find a way to escape the curse. Meanwhile the ministers of the state struggled to comprehend the mystery behind King Parikshit's silence.

As the sun rose over Hastinapur, the grand palace made of brown stones glimmered in its warm rays. It was one of the most magnificent architectural wonders in entire Bharatvarsh. King Parikshit sat in his room, feeling detachment from the life and thinking of renunciation after the recent events. Suddenly, the doorkeeper entered his chamber and exclaimed, " King, the Mahamantri (Prime minister) wishes to meet you urgently." Upon hearing this, he summoned the Mahamantri to his chamber. As soon as the Mahamantri entered, he spoke in a panic-stricken tone, "King, I bring you grave news. Shringi, son of sage Shamik, has cursed you with a death penalty."

After hearing this, Parikshit remained calm and replied with a chuckle, "I will now meet everyone in the court." The Mahamantri immediately convened the meeting, and Parikshit took his place on the throne in the grand Raj darbar. All the ministers in attendance looked worried and distressed. Many were moved to tears, but Parikshit remained stoic and unflustered. He rose to his feet and declared, "I have insulted a sage, and as King, I should be punished with the death penalty. I accept this curse and renounce everything."

The Mahamantri spoke solemnly, saying, "Throughout your reign, you have not committed any act that violates Dharma. You have always been a benevolent ruler, working selflessly for the good of your people. The punishment of death for this one transgression is not justifiable, and this curse is contrary to Dharma." The other ministers also spoke up, saying, "Sage Shamik himself does not wish any harm to come to you. If you are sentenced to death for this, the penance of sages will also be rendered ineffective. Your departure at this time of the beginning of Kaliyuga will harm the entire earth."

Parikshit rose to his feet, "You are all wise and learned. I accept this punishment without any resentment."

The Mahamantri reassured him, "King, every curse has a remedy. This land of Bharatvarsh is home to great sages. Surely, they will find a way." Nevertheless, Parikshit remained resolute, "Death is the ultimate truth. I wish to embrace it without fear." He left everything behind and embarked on the path of renunciation.

Meanwhile, Kaliyuga rejoiced in its success in Manvantar Loka. It had achieved its goal through Anger alone. With Anger gaining strength, Austerity had weakened. Kaliyuga cackled, "Humans are weak. We claimed our first victory. Nothing can prevent us from becoming stronger." Greed, Attachment, and Lust were delighted by this triumph and congratulated Anger on its victory.

The Kuru dynasty was renowned for producing great rulers, but Parikshit had to relinquish his position. His successor, Janmejya, took the throne but the influence of Kaliyuga proved too strong, and the Kuru dynasty began to crumble. With no strong ruler to unite them, Bharatvarsh fragmented into smaller states, each vying for ultimate power. The once-majestic Raj Bhavan of Hastinapur lay in ruins, a mere reminder of a bygone era. As the struggle for power intensified, civil war seemed inevitable.

Amidst the chaotic atmosphere, the Great sages of Bharatvarsh convened a gathering under the leadership of sage named Muni Sahadri. Counted among the great sages of Bharatvarsh and a disciple of the venerable Ved Vyas, Muni Sahadri needed no introduction. He was held in high esteem throughout Bharatvarsh, and despite being hundreds of years old, he was full of youthful enthusiasm. His face shone with radiance, and his long beard and hair, tied at the back of his head, added to his aura. In this time of crisis, only he could devise a strategy that would benefit Bharatvarsh and its people.

The meeting was held in the ashram situated on the Peak of Sumahu Mountain, accessible only to the great sages. The walls of the hermitage were made of huge stones, and the only source of water on the mountain was a spring near the hermitage. Fruit trees and colorful flowers surrounded the ashram, which could only grow in this place. The meeting aimed to discuss the beginning of Kaliyuga and the appointment of the next King of Bharatvarsh and was attended by hundreds of ascetic sages from all over Bharatvarsh. The gathering began with Namaste to the Sun, signaling the start of their quest to find a solution to the problems plaguing Bharatvarsh.

Muni Sahadri spoke up, his eyes scanning the assembly of great sages gathered in the conference. "I thank you all for accepting my invitation and coming to this meeting," he began. "As you are well aware, Bharatvarsh is currently in a state of chaos since Prabhu Shri Krishna's departure and the end of the Kuru dynasty. Kaliyuga is gaining strength day by day, taking advantage of human weakness and turning them into its slaves. But we can stop Kaliyuga with the help of wisdom.

Sage Sujal nodded his head in agreement. "Prabhu Shri Krishna has given us the ultimate wisdom in the form of Gita to reduce the influence of Kaliyuga," he added.

Sage Tejak chimed in, "It is now our duty to spread this knowledge of Gita to the people, but after King Parikshit, Bharatvarsh has not been able to find a worthy ruler. Without a capable king, good governance cannot be established."

Muni Sahadri nodded gravely. "The future of Bharatvarsh will be bleak without a worthy king," he agreed. "We need someone who is powerful, knowledgeable, and dedicated to serving the people. We must search for such a person."

"But will we be able to find such a worthy candidate?" Sage Tejak raised a valid question. "It's rare to find someone who possesses both knowledge and bravery. It's difficult to find someone like that after King Parikshit."

Muni Sahadri held up his hand, silencing the murmurs of doubt in the assembly. "It is possible," he declared. "There must be someone on the land of Bharatvarsh who is worthy of this position. It is decided that we will search for such a person, someone who is not only the best warrior but also the most knowledgeable. This new King will be the one to reduce the influence of Kaliyuga and provide proper governance to Bharatvarsh in these trying times."

5. The Rise of Sakayu Dynasty

In the heart of Bharatvarsh, lay the kingdom of Sakayu ruled by the ambitious King Ketubhan. With the chaos and instability that had plagued the land, Ketubhan saw an opportunity to expand his power and become the supreme ruler of Bharatvarsh. To achieve his goal, he appointed his most skilled and ruthless warrior, Mridant, as his commander.

The first target of their conquest was the state of Chandrapur, located in the north-western region of the land. In a fierce battle, Mridant led the army of Sakayu to victory, defeating the king of Chandrapur and taking control of the state. Ketubhan was overjoyed by this triumph and ordered celebrations throughout his kingdom. Eager to maintain his momentum, Ketubhan summoned an assembly of his top warriors to plan their next move.

With a twirl of his mustache, Ketubhan declared, "Today, I have conquered the majority of Bharatvarsh. And mark my words, the day is not far when I shall reign over the entire land."

Mridant nodded in agreement, "Indeed, it is your foresight that has led to this great feat, King."

Charak, the minister, added, "Without a doubt, My King, your army is the mightiest in all the land. Soon, the whole of Bharatvarsh will be under your rule."

Ketubhan's hunger for power had led him to conquer the eastern and southern states, and he had his sights set on the north. He marched towards Hastinapur, once a great city now in ruins, and rebuilt it as Prasthapur. With his military might, the Sakayu dynasty had seized control of the entire Bharatvarsh.

A grand Raj Bhavan was erected on the banks of the Teesta River, a red masterpiece that drew the awe and admiration of all who saw it. The main gate opened up to a vast green field, leading to a towering building that exuded magnificence and grandeur. It was a sight to behold, a marvel that had no equal in whole of Bharatvarsh.

Ketubhan didn't build this grand Raj Bhavan to serve people, but rather to revel in the luxuries of royal life. With his military might, he forced all the states to bow before him and imposed exorbitant taxes on people to support his massive army. He even began appropriating half of the people's earnings for his own pleasure, plunging Bharatvarsh into the dark ages of Kaliyuga. The position of King, once held in high esteem for its duty to serve the people, has been corrupted into a tool for personal pleasure and indulgence.

Muni Sahadri searched tirelessly for a worthy successor, but the Sakayu dynasty's influence was too great. Many wise sages tried to guide Ketubhan towards a path of righteousness, but he was consumed by the lust for power. Even Muni Sahadri himself attempted to impart the proper principles of governance to Ketubhan, but to no avail.

Ketubhan remained holed up in his grand palace in Prasthapur, swimming in a sea of debauchery and vice. His unquenchable greed had destroyed his conscience, and he was now a slave to the dark forces of Kaliyuga.

The Kaliyuga in Manvantar Loka was elated by the latest development. "We have made incredible progress in such a short amount of time," Kaliyuga proclaimed. "Anger, Greed, Attachment, and Lust are thriving in humans, making us stronger. Soon, we will extend our influence from Manvantar Loka to the entire universe."

Greed chimed in, "You're absolutely right, Kaliyuga! We've ensnared Bharatvarsh, the source of knowledge for the entire planet. We can only be defeated by knowledge, and we've effectively cut off the source of it."

Lust interjected with concern, "But there are still many sages wandering the earth who have transcended our influence through Prabhu Shri Krishna's Gita. They continue to spread knowledge to humans and thwart our plans."

Anger added, "Humans have grown weak. They lack the austerity necessary to resist us. Even Austerity, Compassion, and Love, who are present in our court, remain silent and powerless."

Kaliyuga reassured the group, "We've been successful thus far, and humans are continuing to fall under our control. They'll never be able to overcome us. I am certain that we will become the masters of the entire universe."

The Sakayu dynasty was ruled by greed and violence. The King, blinded by his own power, forgot his responsibilities towards people. Those who didn't bow down before him faced severe consequences. The King imposed heavy taxes on farmers and traders to fill his own treasury, without any regard for their well-being. He had become selfish and only cared about his own pleasures. Despite being aware of the agricultural crisis, he did nothing to improve the situation. Ketubhan, the King, had turned a deaf ear to the wise counsel of Muni Sahadri and had become corrupt with greed. The people of Bharatvarsh were suffering as a result.

Lust, previously dormant, had started to run rampant. Love had been forgotten, and humans were now trapped in the clutches of lust. Men were exploiting women, and women were facing humiliation. Lust had become man's greatest weakness, robbing them of their conscience time and again. In the Sakayu dynasty, Bharatvarsh had been consumed by the darkness of Kaliyuga. The four vices of Kaliyuga, namely Anger, Greed, Lust, and Attachment, had reached their peak in Manvantar Loka. Despite the overwhelming despair, Muni Sahadri refused to give up hope. He firmly believed that there was a capable leader who could restore order and bring prosperity to Bharatvarsh in these troubled times.

6. The Story of the Sinhdham : Tribe in the Himalayas

Deep in the heart of the Himalayan Mountains, nestled amidst snow-capped peaks and crystal-clear rivers, lies the tribe of Sinhdham. The river Stuti flows from the towering snow-capped mountains in the north of the tribe, adding to the breathtaking beauty of the land A paradise of thousands of people, who rely on farming, animal husbandry and the trading of rare medicinal plants. Their swords, crafted with the finest metals, are used in self-defense or to hunt wild animals. But Sinhdham's true strength lies in the unity and love that binds them together. Their assembly of five, elected by the people, governs the tribe with wisdom and fairness. This council comprises of a person in their prime between the ages of 20 to 40, an elder in the age range of 50 to 60 years, another elder aged between 60 to 70 years, a wise woman, and a position reserved for individuals who do not subscribe to traditional gender. Sinhdham is a land of equality, where every child receives a comprehensive education until the age of 18, after which they contribute to the community based on their unique skills. The tribe recognizes no differences based on gender, class or birth. The energy of this tribe is one of peace and holiness, guided by their head, the wise and revered Tethavat.

When Muni Sahadri's attempts to reform Ketubhan failed, he embarked on a treacherous journey with fellow sages to the Himalayas, in search of his dear friend Muni Samved. Both had been disciples of the renowned Ved Vyas and shared a close bond, yet their beliefs about a sage's role in society were starkly different. While Muni Samved shunned worldly pleasures and refused to interfere in politics, Sahadri felt it was his duty to engage with society. Despite their ideological differences, Sahadri knew that Samved was the only *trikaldarshi* left in Bharatvarsh, possessing the knowledge of all three times.

As the group of sages trekked towards the towering peak of Kantak in the Himalayas, they were ambushed by a ferocious pack of hungry hyenas. Despite the sages attempts to show them love and kindness, the wild beasts only hungered for their flesh. Sages found themselves defenseless and unable to escape the predators' grasp. But hope arrived in the form of a courageous young man, who charged in with his sword drawn and took on the hyenas with fearless vigor. His bravery prevailed, and the hyenas fled before his might. The sages were saved, and they all thanked the valiant hero. Muni Sahadri gazed upon the young man in awe, taking in his towering height, broad shoulders, long hair, shining sword, and radiant face.

Muni Sahadri looked at the young man and said, "Young man, thank you very much. What are you doing in this forest?" The young man greeted everyone with "Namaste" and replied, "Our tribe, Sinhdham, lies nearby. We often visit the forest. You are all welcome to visit our tribe."

Sages accepted the invitation and followed the young man. Curious, Muni Sahadri asked for the young man's name, to which he replied politely, "My name is Vatsalya."

As the group arrived at the Sinhdham tribe, the evening had cast a reddish hue over the sky. Herds of grazing animals were making their way back to the tribe. The people of the tribe were busy with their daily chores. Upon seeing the sages, they gathered to welcome them. Tethavat, the head of the tribe, came to the main gate and extended his warm welcome to the sages, escorting them to the guest house. The sages were served with fruits and milk, and the tribe ensured that no aspect of hospitality was left unfulfilled.

Muni Sahadri sensed a positive and divine energy in the air of this mystical tribe, something he did not expect to find in a forest tribe. He asked Tethavat about this unique aura and the reason behind it. Tethavat looked around at the gathered sages and began his tale. " Hundreds of years ago, our tribe belonged to the plunderers. We used to rob the travelers on our way and sustain our lives. Once, the people of our tribe encountered a sage. They asked him for wealth. The sage humbly stated that he was only a sage and knowledge was his wealth. The people of our tribe showed him the fear of death, but he remained undeterred. Our tribe witnessed for the first time a person who was not afraid of death. At that moment, the people of our tribe brought him along.

The sages listened with rapt attention as Tethavat continued. "That night, sage shared the epic tale of Ramayana, and the impact it had on our people was indescribable. Everyone was moved to tears, and from that moment on, We began to follow in the footsteps of ideal king Shri Ram. He became our inspiration, our ideal."

Tethavat's voice grew softer as he continued his story. "The Sage stayed in this tribe, and day after day, he shared with us more knowledge, teaching us about Prabhu Shri Krishna and the Gita. And in the end, he transformed us.

We abandoned our old ways, and began to live our lives guided by the wisdom he had shared with us."

Muni Sahadri's heart swelled with wonder and emotion as Tethavat recounted the incredible story of their tribe's transformation from ruthless robbers to righteous devotees of ideal King Shri Ram. "Who was that sage who brought such divine light into your lives?" Sahadri asked eagerly.

"His name was Sage Sayunkta," Tethavat replied with reverence. Sahadri's eyes widened in awe. "Sage Sayunkta of the Dwapar era! Your tribe was blessed to have him among you." Tethavat nodded, "Indeed, it is thanks to him that we have been able to keep this tribe free from the corrupting influence of Kaliyuga."

Muni Sahadri and other sages stayed for a week at Sinhdham. Every day, the sages regaled the people of the tribe with new and enlightening stories, while Vatsalya, a young warrior of the tribe, stood guard, ensuring the safety of their esteemed guests.

As the time came for the sages to bid farewell and make their way back to the Himalayas, the tribe gathered to bestow their blessings and gratitude upon them. And Vatsalya, along with other brave warriors of the tribe, accompanied the sages, safeguarding their journey. Muni Sahadri, in particular, struck up a conversation with Vatsalya and was struck by his admirable qualities and courage.

Sahadri asked Vatsalya, "What is the greatest knowledge you have acquired thus far?"

Vatsalya responded, "The knowledge of oneself is the greatest knowledge, and the Gita is the best book to gain such knowledge." The sages were pleased to hear his answer.

Sahadri then asked Vatsalya about the impact of Kaliyuga. Vatsalya responded, "The people of our tribe are not aware of it, but as long as humanity remains on the right path and is knowledgeable, Kaliyuga will be powerless. Our flaws are its food."

As the group rested, Vatsalya and his companions went to gather food. Sage Tej praised Vatsalya's wisdom and dedication, despite his youth.

Muni Sahadri spoke, "The arrival of sage Sayunkta to this place cannot be a mere coincidence. He must have had a reason for coming here. This tribe appears to be a *Satyapunj* in the dark age of Kaliyuga."

Sage Utsuk expressed his thoughts, "The knowledge and prowess of Vatsalya should not be confined to this tribe alone."

Soon after, Vatsalya and the other warriors came back with fruits from the forest, which they offered to the sages. Muni Sahadri then instructed Vatsalya and his companions to return to their tribe. Despite Vatsalya's insistence on accompanying them, Muni Sahadri refused, and they obeyed his order.

Subsequently, Muni Sahadri and the other sages set off towards Kantak peak, where they encountered Muni Samved.

7. The Chosen One: A Quest for the Betterment of Bharatvarsh

Upon his return from the Himalayas after having discussed with his esteemed friend Muni Samved, Muni Sahadri, accompanied by a cohort of other venerable sages, made their way to the kingdom of Pratipur, located in the southernmost tip of Bharatvarsh, nestled upon the shores of the great ocean. At that juncture, Pratipur stood as the solitary state in all Bharatvarsh, whose people experienced contentment under the rule of their king. King Jayavardhan, though devoted to the betterment of his people, remained bereft of the capability to challenge Ketubhan, the incumbent King of Bharatvarsh. King Jayavardhan was filled with a sense of elation upon hearing of Muni Sahadri's arrival. Welcomed with great fervour at the palace, Muni Sahadri and the other revered sages were received with utmost reverence by him.

(In assembly of Pratipur)

Muni Sahadri addressed King Jayavardhan with a profound proclamation - nestled in the lap of the Himalayas lies a tribe named Sinhdham, where the energy of the Satyuga is palpable even in the Kaliyuga era. King Jayavardhan, taken aback by the statement, responded with great elation, remarking how pleased he was to learn that such a place existed on Earth where the Satyuga's essence could be experienced.

Upon hearing the praise bestowed upon the tribe named Sinhdham, other sages and seers also extolled its virtues. Following their remarks, Muni Sahadri turned his gaze towards King Jayavardhan and gravely proclaimed,

"This tribe is akin to the Sun illuminating the darkness, and nestled within its embrace lies the energy of the Satyuga. Therein resides a youth named Vatsalya. I beseech thee, my liege, to extend an invitation to him to come to Pratipur."

Jayavardhan, taken aback by the sage's impassioned plea, queried, "What makes this youth so special?"

To this, Muni Sahadri replied, "I simply implore you to meet him once. "

Jayavardhan, intrigued by the sage's words, declared, "Your words have piqued my curiosity, and I shall certainly meet this Vatsalya."

Then, as per the orders of the Muni Sahadri, King Jayavardhan sent his envoy with an invitation.

Meanwhile, Vatsalya was preoccupied with fulfilling his daily duties. He was appointed to ensure the safety of the tribe and was soon to be appointed as the chief of the tribe's warriors.

No one knew about Vatsalya's birthplace and parents, he arrived in the tribe's midst as a wailing, three-year-old in the dark of night. Despite the tribe's best efforts to locate his parents, they failed to uncover any trace of the mysterious child's origin. It was then speculated that Vatsalya's parents may have been hunted and killed by wild animals, while he alone miraculously survived to find refuge in the tribe's care. Thus, the tribe adopted the orphaned boy, and over time, the tribe's collective heart swelled with love and affection for their new member. Forgetting his past, he grew up alongside other children in the affection of this mystical tribe.

In the same tribe, there was a girl named Sugandha who loved him. She and Vatsalya grew up together in their childhood. Sugandha had a special affection for him. In their youth, this affection turned into pure love. Vatsalya was soon to be appointed as the chief warrior, and afterwards, he and Sugandha were going to be bound in the bond of marriage. The whole tribe knew about their holy love and they were eagerly awaiting their wedding.

During this time, the envoy sent by Jayavardhan arrived at the tribe. He introduced himself to the people of the tribe and they welcomed him warmly. The ambassador was amazed by the grandeur of the tribe and began to inquire about Vatsalya. When Sugandha heard about the envoy then she came to meet him filled with curiosity.

She looked towards the envoy and asked, "Sir, may I know the purpose of your visit?"

The envoy replied, "Madam, my name is Kalp. I am an ambassador of King Jayavardhan of Pratipur kingdom and have come with a letter for Vatsalya. This letter has been sent by Muni Sahadri."

The moment the people of the mystical tribe heard the name "Muni Sahadri," their eyes sparkled with excitement. They quickly gathered around Kalp, their esteemed guest, and led him to a grand guest chamber with utmost reverence. Just then, the tribe head Tethavat, a wise and powerful figure, arrived and greeted Kalp. With a reassuring smile, he spoke, "Vatsalya has ventured to the northern side of the majestic Himalayas and will return by evening. For now, dear guest, please make yourself at home and rest."

The people of the tribe were ecstatic upon hearing the newsletter. They gathered in the evening, sitting under the twinkling stars and surrounded by the warm glow of the fire.

They danced to the rhythmic beats of the tribal music, and Kalp was mesmerized by the sheer beauty of it all.

As the sound of hooves approached, Vatsalya and his companions arrived at the ceremony, dressed in their formidable warrior garb. The assembly fell silent, eagerly awaiting the message from Kalp. Tethavat, the tribe head, explained to Vatsalya about Kalp's arrival, and Vatsalya took his place among the gathering. With a nod from Tethavat, Kalp began to read out the message.

"I bring you this missive from Muni Sahadri at the behest of King Jayavardhan," Kalp announced. "Muni Sahadri pays tribute to the Sinhdam tribe under Tethavat's guidance. I was greatly impressed by this tribe during my travels. The knowledge and valour of the tribe's people are commendable. Their love for each other is without any selfish motive, and my heart is filled with joy upon seeing this. Walking in the footsteps of ideal King Shri Ram and Prabhu Krishna, your tribe is a source of inspiration for the entire Bharatvarsh. I am greatly influenced by my encounter with Vatsalya. He is both wise and a great warrior. Therefore, I invite him to Pratipur. I have full faith that you will accept my request and send him there."

Upon hearing this letter, the people of the tribe were both surprised and delighted. Tethavat, with a worried expression, said, "We must respect Muni Sahadri's order.

In response, Vatsalya rose to his feet with unwavering determination, pledging his loyalty to Muni Sahadri, a man he held in high esteem. Sugandha, upon hearing this declaration, excused herself from the gathering, her heart heavy with emotion. As the night wore on and the tribe dispersed after the meal, Vatsalya sought out Sugandha.

Sugandha was seated by the tranquil banks of the Stuti river, a familiar spot where she and Vatsalya would often meet. The moon's radiant glow illuminated the surroundings with a golden hue, while a gentle breeze from the snow-capped mountains mingled with the soothing sound of the flowing river, creating a serene ambiance. Perched on a massive rock, Sugandha felt the cool water caress her face, wiping away her tears.

Just then, Vatsalya emerged and settled down beside her. He gazed at Sugandha with concern and asked, "Why did you leave the assembly? You haven't even had your meal."

Amidst her tears, Sugandha tightly embraced Vatsalya, exclaiming, "You won't come back from there."

Vatsalya returned her embrace, gently reassuring her, "I have been called for a specific task. But I will come back after accomplishing it."

Sugandha expressed her fears, "The pleasures of Raj Bhavan may sway you, and you might find someone else."

Vatsalya gazed into her eyes with sincerity, and declared, "You know me well. The luxuries of Raj Bhavan cannot distract me, and I cannot imagine anyone else by my side except you."

Sugandha clung to him, her grip tight and her doubts evident in her eyes. "I don't believe you," she whispered, her voice choked with emotion.

Vatsalya gently cupped her face in his hands, his eyes unwavering. "I consider ideal King Shri Ram as my inspiration," he declared solemnly. "I will marry only you. That is my promise."

Upon hearing his unwavering vow, Sugandha's fears and worries seemed to melt away. A sense of calm washed over her as she looked into Vatsalya's eyes, reassured by his resolute words. She could feel the sincerity in his voice, and her heart swelled with love and trust.

Next day, As the golden rays of the rising sun illuminated the sky, Vatsalya set out on his journey to Pratipur, accompanied by Kalp. Sugandha had prepared a hearty meal and packed fruits for the journey, which Vatsalya gratefully accepted. Clad in his formidable warrior attire, wielding his sword and shield, he mounted his horse with determination and embarked on the adventure.

The mountain paths proved treacherous, testing Vatsalya's skills and resilience. But after a few days of challenging travel, they descended onto the coastal plains of the river Sangya. Vatsalya couldn't help but look back at the towering mountains with a sense of nostalgia, missing his tribe and Sugandha. However, he shook off the emotions and focused on his mission. With each passing day, he pushed forward with unwavering resolve. After a week-long journey, Vatsalya and Kalp finally arrived at Pratipur.

The white Raj Bhavan stood proudly on the shores of the vast ocean, surrounded by verdant greenery. Its circular pillars held up the grand structure, and as soon as Vatsalya stepped inside, he caught the attention of Princess Vaidehi, who was standing on the second floor of the Raj Bhavan. Vaidehi was renowned for her unparalleled beauty, and her allure was truly captivating. However, she was also a formidable warrior, which deterred any man from making advances towards her. Despite Vaidehi's attraction towards Vatsalya, he only saw her as a visitor.

A mere observer, I watched him with awe,
A certain charm within him that I saw,
Unwittingly, I fell under his spell,
Convinced of his worth, a tale to tell.
His eyes, they wandered not towards me,
It made me question my own allure,

Kalp escorted Vatsalya to the guest chamber, where he arranged for refreshments and food. As Vatsalya sat down, Kalp hurried to the Pratipur Raj Bhavan to inform Muni Sahadri and King Jayavardhan about Vatsalya's arrival.

Upon hearing the news, Muni Sahadri was thrilled, and even King Jayavardhan was intrigued about why a young man from a distant tribe was invited. Both of them came to personally meet Vatsalya. Vatsalya was sitting in the guest chamber, and from upstairs, Muni Sahadri and King Jayavardhan came to see him.

King Jayavardhan took a good look at him and commented, "This young man is brimming with brilliance, but why is he dressed so simply? What is it about him that you have called him from such a faraway place?"

Muni Sahadri replied with conviction, "This young man possesses prodigious talent that he himself is unaware of. He is destined to be the next King of Bharatvarsh."

Jayavardhan was surprised and replied, "You are knowledgeable, but I doubt your statement. He does not come from a royal family, nor does he have an army, nor does he seems ambitious. How can he become a king just by being a knowledgeable and skilled warrior?"

Muni Sahadri responded, "In this kaliyuga, the ruler of Bharatvarsh should not belong to a royal family. Putting an end to dynasty-based rule is necessary. Only then can the foundation of Kaliyuga be weakened." After this, Muni Sahadri and king Jayavardhan went to meet Vatsalya.

As Vatsalya stood up and bowed down, Muni Sahadri expressed his gratitude for coming in response to his message. Vatsalya humbly replied, " Your message is an order for me. You command me."

King Jayavardhan observed Vatsalya's innocence, and his doubts regarding Muni Sahadri's statement increased. He then addressed Vatsalya and said, "Muni Sahadri was praising you a lot. He seems to have a high regard for your tribe." Vatsalya bowed his head in gratitude and thanked Jayavardhan.

Then, Vatsalya looked towards Muni Sahadri and asked, "For what purpose have I been called? Please give me your orders."

Muni Sahadri replied, "You seem eager to know. Listen carefully, Bharatvarsh is currently ruled by the Sakayu dynasty, and they are exploiting the people. Ketubhan sits on the throne solely based on his army's power. In the past, we had rulers like ideal King Shri Ram and the Kuru dynasty who admirably performed their duties as rulers. In Kaliyuga, only a virtuous person who is knowledgeable and skilled in warfare should become King. Ketubhan is not eligible to be the King of Bharatvarsh. I want you to dethrone him."

Vatsalya's mind raced with questions as he processed Muni Sahadri's request. "Why me?" he finally asked, his voice trembling with curiosity.

"Because only you can complete this task," Muni Sahadri replied, his eyes filled with confidence. Vatsalya nodded, understanding the gravity of the situation. "But killing Ketubhan alone won't bring about the change we need," he stated matter-of-factly. "There will a fierce war for dethroning Sakayu dynast and for that we need an army."

Muni Sahadri smiled, impressed by Vatsalya's insight. "That's why we have called upon you," he explained. "You will have the necessary resources to achieve this goal."

"But Jayavardhan's doubt still lingered as he questioned Vatsalya's abilities, asking skeptically, "Can you do this?"

Vatsalya remained completely calm in the face of doubt. At that moment, Muni Sahadri intervened and said, "Contemplate and inform us of your decision as soon as possible. Before making any decision, it is important to understand that we are doing this for the welfare of the entire Bharatvarsh. "

"Muni Sahadri and King Jayavardhan departed, leaving Vatsalya deep in thought. Meanwhile, Vaidehi, who had heard of Vatsalya from Kalp, found herself deeply intrigued by the young man. When she learned that Muni Sahadri had summoned Vatsalya, her curiosity grew even stronger. As the evening wore on, Vatsalya mulled over Muni Sahadri's words, while Jayavardhan fretted that Vatsalya would be too afraid to carry out the mission, and Muni Sahadri remained hopeful.

The next day, Vatsalya strode into the grand royal court, his eyes filled with determination as he stood before Muni Sahadri and King Jayavardhan. 'Before I begin the task you've given me,' he said, "I would like to know more about King Ketubhan of the Sakayu dynasty and his governance system. "

Muni Sahadri and king Jayavardhan were taken aback by Vatsalya's request, but they agreed to fill him in. Jayavardhan then explained, 'There is an annual conference of all the states under King Ketubhan, and this year's conference is to be held in Prasthapur. At the conference, Ketubhan will discuss his policies with the kings of each state under his rule. Jayavardhan had already decided to send his successor, Princess Vaidehi, to the conference, but now he also decided to send Vatsalya along with her.

Vaidehi, who had recently been appointed as the heiress of Pratipur, was making preparations to depart for Prasthapur as per the original schedule. However, her plans took a sudden turn when king Jayavardhan informed her about Vatsalya and instructed her to take Vatsalya along to Prasthapur. Vaidehi was filled with curiosity and eagerness to meet Vatsalya. Upon receiving the king's command, she felt inwardly delighted and expressed her desire to meet Vatsalya.

King Jayavardhan responded, "You can meet him as per your desire."

That very night, In the southern wing of the palace, Vaidehi, the newly appointed ruler of Pratipur, summoned Vatsalya to meet her in the grand chamber. The spacious room was filled with various armaments and weapons, but amidst it all, Vaidehi sat alone with her tresses flowing in waves. She wore a silver hoop on her comely nose, and her full bosom glowed, with her bare abdomen revealing her navel. Her lower limbs were exposed to the gusts of wind blowing in from the ocean beyond the doorway. As Vatsalya prostrated himself before the princess, he was struck by her unconventional attire. However, Vaidehi returned his obeisance and looked deep into his eyes. In a bewitching tone, she welcomed him, "Vatsalya, you are most welcome. King Jayavardhan has ordered us to go to Prasthapur together. I have summoned you here so that we may converse beforehand." Bowing again, she leaned forward to accentuate the fullness of her bosom and continued, "But first, you must understand me." Vatsalya chuckled, and Vaidehi, stepping closer, queried, "What would you like to know about the Sakayu dynasty?"

Vatsalya remained focused on his mission and did not allow himself to be ensnared by Vaidehi's charms. He replied, "Princess, I want to know about the structure of the Sakayu dynasty. Muni Sahadri has tasked me to dethrone Ketubhan from his post."

Vaidehi asked, "How do you plan to accomplish this?" Vatsalya responded, "I will first meet Ketubhan and then decide. I have to pursue my goals on my own. There is no certainty of success in following someone else's guidance." Vaidehi looked into Vatsalya's eyes, which conveyed both innocence and truth. She was astonished and admiring of his ability to resist her allure. She said, "Look at the beauty waiting for you before you defeat the dynasty."

Vatsalya laughed and replied, "Princess, please don't test me. I can see that your wisdom and warrior spirit are not hidden behind a veil of lust." Vaidehi smiled in amazement and asked, "How did you know? No one has ever been able to escape my trap before." You are the first,"

Vaidehi said with a smile. "Upon seeing you, I felt that lust cannot dominate you. There is something different about you that others lack. One who can conquer lust can achieve anything."

Vatsalya looked at Vaidehi but did not utter a word. Vaidehi then dressed herself, casting a surreptitious glance at Vatsalya, and started demonstrating her collection of weaponry to him. Vatsalya was attentively captivated as Vaidehi expressed her belief that only a worthy King should rule Bharatvarsh, and that the Sakayu dynasty was not up to the task. It was not a well-wisher of the people, and therefore had to be ousted in the interest of the nation.

Vatsalya responded politely, "He is still ruler of Bharatvarsh. It is crucial for us to comprehend his system of governance and familiarize ourselves with his strengths and weaknesses.

Vaidehi found Vatsalya's assertion fitting and couldn't help but smile as she looked at him. Her eyes clearly displayed her admiration towards Vatsalya. The following day, they embarked on a journey to Prasthapur together.

8. The Rise of Vatsalya: A Tale of Courage and Victory

Princess Vaidehi and Vatsalya rode on their horses, leading a convoy of hundreds of soldiers as they made their way towards Prasthapur. The journey was treacherous, their path winding through rugged valleys and rushing rivers. Amidst the breathtaking beauty of nature, Vaidehi and Vatsalya engaged in deep discussions about the current state of governance in Bharatvarsh. They talked about the issues that plagued the land, and debated possible solutions.

As evening drew near, their convoy approached a high ghat, surrounded by lush green fields and the gentle sound of a nearby spring. Massive trees lined the road, their branches swaying in the cool breeze and refreshing the travelers' faces.

Princess Vaidehi and Vatsalya's bond grew stronger as they embarked on this difficult journey towards Prasthapur. As Vaidehi gazed at the stunning scenery surrounding them, she couldn't help but express her admiration to Vatsalya. "You live in the midst of natural beauty in your tribe," she said, her lips curling up into a slight smile. "What a blissful atmosphere."

Vatsalya, a man of few words, simply replied, "Yes, Princess."

Vaidehi's smile faded as she corrected him, "You should address me not as Princess, but simply as Vaidehi."

"I hold great respect for you," Vatsalya explained.

Unconvinced, Vaidehi sharply interrupted him, "Muni Sahadri himself summoned you here to overthrow the

Sakayu dynasty from power, and I share that very goal. Together, we shall achieve it. There is no need for unnecessary formalities."

Vatsalya couldn't help but chuckle at Vaidehi's modesty. "Alright, Vaidehi!" he replied, amused. "But why do you desire to dethrone the Sakayu dynasty? Do you aspire to become the King of Bharatvarsha?"

Vaidehi's responded firmly, "I am not greedy for the position of King". Sakayu King Ketubhan is not the protector of Bharatvarsh. His actions are nothing but robbery, which is unacceptable. The ruler of Bharatvarsh should be like our ideal King Shri Ram, who ruled without any selfishness.

She continued, "Bharatvarsh is a land of great wisdom. Its ruler should be a public servant, not a robber. Today, we are the richest country in the world, and we possess vast knowledge. We must continue to progress in this direction. The path to the welfare of the entire world runs through Bharatvarsh, but it cannot be achieved if the Sakayu dynasty remains in power."

Vatsalya listened intently to Vaidehi's words, nodding in agreement. "Your aim is truly great and selfless," he said, admiration evident in his voice. "You will be successful because you are fighting to end the Sakayu dynasty not for your own interests, but for the welfare of people of this country."

Vaidehi's gaze softened as she looked at Vatsalya. "What about you?" she asked gently. "How do you envision the King of Bharatvarsh?"

Vatsalya's eyes gleamed with a quiet intensity. "Every King of Bharatvarsh should be like ideal King Shri

Ram," he replied firmly." He has been the most inspirational King in our history, and every king should aspire to follow in his footsteps."

Vaidehi smiled, pleased with Vatsalya's response. "Why have you chosen to join me on this journey?" she asked curiously.

Vatsalya said, "I believe that my aspirations will align with my purpose on this journey." Vaidehi's gaze met Vatsalya's as she asserted, "By my side, you will undoubtedly realize your purpose."

They arrived at the Ghat mound for the evening, where they shared a meal and retired to their respective quarters. While the soldiers found rest in their pavilions, Vaidehi struggled to find solace in her own. Tossing and turning in distress, she eventually abandoned her efforts to sleep and ventured outside to bask in the splendor of the sky. Her hair whipped about in the chilly winds as she roamed the verdant field with folded hands. Suddenly, Vaidehi caught a glimpse of Vatsalya lying at a distance, gazing up at the stars. Delighted by his presence, she wordlessly crept up to him and lay down beside him. Despite her attempts at stealth, Vatsalya was aware of her presence.

"Do you not fear lying on the ground like this?" Vaidehi asked, peering at him.

Vatsalya chuckled and replied, "I can feel the energy of the elements from which I am made. It brings me satisfaction. What are you afraid of?"

"Fear of snakes and scorpions," Vaidehi replied.

Vatsalya encouraged her to forget her fears and embrace the fast-blowing, cool breeze, the trees that took on different shapes, the skyscraping mountains, and the twinkling stars in the sky, all visible from the very earth they lay on. Vaidehi joined him in laughter, before turning to ask, "What else do you like?"

Vatsalya turned his gaze towards Vaidehi, and she looked back at him. Her body was like a masterpiece of geometric curves, from head to toe. Vatsalya smiled and said, "I have taken a liking to you. Your humbleness, selflessness, and fearlessness are all qualities that I admire. Vatsalya knew the inner beauty of Vaidehi - the beauty that lies within Vaidehi which was many times more beautiful than her body - which was much more beautiful than her physical appearance.

After hearing Vatsalya's compliment, Vaidehi felt shy and turned to lie on her back, looking up at the starry sky. "I only behave like this with you," she admitted. "Everyone else is afraid of me."

Vatsalya asked, "Why do you behave differently to me?"

"Because you are pure-hearted and good," Vaidehi replied with a smile. "You have conquered lust." They both burst out laughing and spent the night under the stars.

The next day, they arrived at Kinchal clan, a farming community located on the border of Pratipur's kingdom. As soon as the news of Vaidehi's arrival spread, hundreds of farmers gathered to meet her. Vatsalya followed behind her as she went around meeting everyone.

The farmers expressed their grievances about the atrocities committed by the royal dynasty. "The King takes more than half of our grain in the name of taxes," one farmer complained. "We struggle to produce enough to sell, and even when we do, we don't receive a fair price," another farmer shared his story.

"Many of us have committed suicide," added another farmer. "Our condition is getting worse day by day, and no one seems to care about us."

Vaidehi listened to their stories and comforted them, offering financial help as well.

After their interaction with the farmers, Vatsalya and Vaidehi resumed their journey. Vaidehi confided in Vatsalya, revealing that the Kinchal king, under the instruction of Ketubhan, was exploiting and oppressing the people of his state. Despite her awareness of the situation, she felt powerless to intervene and bring about a change.

Vatsalya reassured Vaidehi, "No one can exploit the people for long and continue to rule."

Vaidehi declared with determination, "We will soon end the Sakayu dynasty and put a worthy person on the throne of Bharatvarsh."

While continuing their journey, they encountered several abandoned schools with a declining numbers of student. Vatsalya learnt that the Sakayu dynasty considered education expenditure as a burden on their treasury and actively discouraged people from acquiring knowledge, solely to preserve their power. Even wise sages had forsaken their roles as educators and sought alternative livelihoods.

Ketubhan was known everywhere for his oppressive rule. Extortion and plunder were on the rise, and there was no provision of justice for the people. The values that defined Bharatvarsh were now losing their significance. While some people saw Ketubhan as the root of the problem, others attributed it to the dark age of Kaliyuga. The hope for a worthy king to lead Bharatvarsh was fading fast under Ketubhan's rule, and the land was headed towards a dark abyss.

Ketubhan implemented the zamindari system to exploit the people. This system ensured that all property belonged to the king and was handled by his landlords, who were nothing but robbers. Other kings in the Sakayu dynasty followed Ketubhan's lead. Also, the standard of health services was deteriorating rapidly. Wealth had become the determinant of access to healthcare, and the people lived in fear and oppression. Vatsalya was deeply moved by the suffering of the people and felt immense sympathy for them.

Their journey brought them to Chitrapur, a beautiful city on the banks of the Teesta River. The city was a sight to behold, and nature's beauty was on full display. The convoy stopped for rest, and everyone was provided with an inn that overlooked the river. Vaidehi and Vatsalya were delighted with the view from their grand inn, as the blue waters of the Teesta River stretched out before them. The sun was setting, and the sky turned red. Birds were flying back to their nests, and golden-colored deer were drinking from the river. The lush green surroundings spread love and beauty all around.

Vaidehi's heart leaped with joy as she gazed upon the breathtaking scene before her. Without a moment's hesitation, she rushed towards Vatsalya 's chambers, eager to share this enchanting sight with him. As she led him to the outer door, she exclaimed, "I have never been so happy! The sound of the flowing river brings me such joy!"

Vatsalya, who had been watching her with wonder, could not help but admire her radiance. "Nature is indeed beautiful," Vaidehi continued, lost in the splendor of the moment.

"You are no less beautiful than nature," Vatsalya said to her. "Always wear that jewel of a smile."

Vaidehi blushed at his compliment, tying her hair back nervously. "Do I not look good without a smile?" she asked.

"Not as much as nature," Vatsalya replied.

After spending a while taking in the stunning scenery, they settled down for dinner and discussed the upcoming convention in Prasthapur. They were tired due to the journey of several days. A cool breeze flowed through the large doors of the inn, and they both fell asleep in the same bed."

It was morning. Vaidehi found herself in Vatsalya's bed. She began to feel embarrassed. Vatsalya had already awakened and was greeting the Sun with Namaste. Vaidehi removed the blanket from herself and slowly approached Vatsalya, fumbling and said, "I don't even know when I fell asleep." While talking, she kept lowering her eyes repeatedly, and the pace of her breathing was showing her restlessness.

"Why feel ashamed?" Vatsalya reassured her, flashing a charming grin. "A smile suits you better."

Vaidehi couldn't help but giggle, and they set off towards Prasthapur, eager to continue their journey together.

Nestled in the northernmost part of Bharatvarsh lay the grand city of Prasthapur, its towering red buildings beckoning to visitors from far and wide. The circular pillars of the city shone brilliantly in the sunlight, a sight to behold for anyone who gazed upon them. As the time for the convention drew near, the entire city donned its festive attire, adorned with intricate decorations and vibrant colors. On arrival in this grand city, Vaidehi wore her regal garments, ready to take her place among the assembly.

Amidst the grand circular building, every seat was arranged with utmost precision as many kings of states gathered, all of whom were under the rule of Ketubhan. These states paid their taxes on time, and in return, Ketubhan refrained from interfering in their internal affairs. As the dignitaries engaged in animated discussions, Ketubhan, the middle-aged ruler of the land, arrived in his diamond-studded robes. His long and thick nose, along with his protruding stomach, revealed his love for feasts.

Surrounded by his loyal bodyguards, the king addressed the assembly, and every person in the room stood up to show their respect. "Welcome, everyone!" proclaimed Ketubhan. "I have united Bharatvarsh in Kaliyuga and saved it from disintegration. It is because of me that Bharatvarsh exists today."

The mood shifted as Ketubhan's tone turned serious. He reminded the assembly that they paid less tax and that the taxes collected were no longer enough to support the kingdom's needs. Turning towards Vaidehi, the Princess of Pratipur, he accused her state of paying the least taxes.

Quickly rising to her feet, Vaidehi defended herself, "King! Our expenditure is more in the welfare of the people, and at present, we are spending the maximum on farmers. We are giving you tax in the proper proportion only."

But Ketubhan remained unyielding, "I have nothing to do with your expenditure. Reduce expenditure on education and farmers. All other states except yours, pay double tax." The tension in the room mounted as Ketubhan's words echoed through the circular building, leaving every king to ponder their next move.

As Vaidehi began to speak, Ketubhan interrupted her, commanding her to remain calm. "Most of Bharatvarsh is under my governance," he boasted. "I have implemented the practice of zamindari, which has proven to be a great source of revenue. And to ensure that any rebellion is crushed immediately, I have provided soldiers to the landlords. People will pay taxes according to the king's orders, not their own whims. My army is powerful and huge in numbers and Mridant, my commander, will attest to its power."

Mridant stood up with great pride, declaring, "Even if all the military powers of the states were combined, your military power would still surpass theirs by many times. We can destroy any state with just one order of our King. And with new arms factories being set up every year, our army is the largest in the history of Bharatvarsh."

Vaidehi was undaunted by their warnings. "This army is meant to protect our nation, not to intimidate us," she stated firmly.

Now another king Nivedak warned her, "Princess, your kingdom exists only at the will of King Ketubhan."

Vaidehi replied, "We are not under anyone's control."

Ketubhan grew angry and threatened, "Pratipur may be on the southern end of the country, but it is not beyond my reach. I spared it because of my old friendship with your father. But if you run this state, I will consider attacking it. Tell your father that he must now pay double taxes. Now, you will only listen in this assembly."

The assembly listened in silence as King Vrinha acquiesced, "King, we understand your wishes. We will double the taxes and implement the zamindari system."

Vatsalya watched from the sidelines like a spectator. As the evening progressed, King Ketubhan organized a cultural program featuring dancers that left everyone entranced. Alcohol flowed freely, fueling the lustful fascination with the swaying hips of the performers. Even the army officers couldn't resist the allure of the dancers, becoming increasingly excited as the night went on. When this lustful event ended, everyone returned to their respective states.

Ketubhan urged the states under his control to loot their people, perpetuating his own greed. Vaidehi was deeply disappointed by what she had witnessed but felt powerless to do anything about it. She and Vatsalya returned to Pratipur, where they were summoned by Muni Sahadri for a discussion.

Jayavardhan turned to Vatsalya, "You've just come from meeting Ketubhan. What have you decided?"

Vatsalya responded calmly, "King, I will fight this war. Ketubhan is not fit to rule Bharatvarsh, and I will defeat him."

Vaidehi stood by his side, elated by his resolve.

Muni Sahadri exclaimed, "Excellent!"

Jayavardhan asked, "But what will be your strategy?"

Vatsalya, "I want ten thousand warriors."

Jayavardhan expressed concern, "But Ketubhan's army is in the lakhs. Will you be able to defeat them?"

Vatsalya responded confidently, "The objective of the war for army is of utmost importance. Ketubhan's soldiers have become selfish and forgotten their patriotism. My purpose is to free Bharatvarsh from these robbers. With ten times fewer soldiers, I can still defeat them."

Jayavardhan was impressed by his resolve, and Muni Sahadri agreed, "Vatsalya, we must win this war. You devise a strategy, and we will provide you with warriors."

As Vatsalya and Vaidehi left the meeting together, she couldn't help but feel overjoyed that he had finally decided to take on Ketubhan. She longed to embrace him but hesitated. Walking beside him, Vaidehi couldn't help but wonder how he planned to defeat their enemy with such a small army.

"I told in front of king Jayavardhan," Vatsalya replied confidently.

Vaidehi chuckled. "You told the truth. I alone could take on hundreds of soldiers."

"I have no doubt about your war skills," Vatsalya assured her.

Meanwhile, in the royal court of Pratipur, Muni Sahadri and King Jayavardhan discussed the possibility of Vatsalya's success in the upcoming war.

"Of course he can succeed," Sahadri declared.

"What makes you so confident?" Jayavardhan inquired.

"This is the purpose of his life, which he has finally realized," Sahadri explained.

Jayavardhan offered his support. "I can provide warriors for him, but Pratipur will be directly involved in this war."

Sahadri reassured him. "Don't worry. He will win."

"On your advice, I am willing to put all the resources of my state into this war," Jayavardhan declared.

"Stop worrying, King," Sahadri said.

In a short amount of time, Jayavardhan had rallied skilled warriors from Pratipur and surrounding states to join the fight against Ketubhan's immoral rule. The warriors, armed and ready, had gathered at a secret location as per Jayavardhan's orders. In attendance were Jayavardhan, Muni Sahadri, Vatsalya, and Vaidehi.

Jayavardhan addressed the assembly. "We all know that Ketubhan's rule is nothing short of tyranny. His actions are unacceptable, and the people of Bharatvarsh are suffering as a result. It's time we dispose him of power, and that's why we're here today."

The assembled warriors erupted in congratulatory cheers.

Muni Sahadri added his support. "I agree with King's statement. Ketubhan's rule is a product of the dark virtues of Kaliyuga, and he's causing untold suffering to the people. This war is about establishing justice and righteousness. It is a noble cause."

Vaidehi was thrilled to hear these addresses from Jayavardhan and Muni Sahadri. In the midst of the gathering, Muni Sahadri asked Vatsalya to address the warriors.

Vatsalya, a stranger to the assembly, surveyed the crowd for a few moments before suddenly stepping forward, brandishing his sword. "I've heard that you all are the best warriors," he said. "I challenge anyone who considers themselves a skilled fighter to come forward and face me."

The entire assembly fell silent, stunned by Vatsalya's boldness. Jayavardhan was taken aback, and even Vaidehi was filled with wonder. But then, Vayuvraj, renowned as the best sword fighter in the land, stepped forward to accept Vatsalya's challenge.

The battle was intense, the sound of clashing steel echoing through the gathering. Both warriors were skilled, but Vatsalya's lightning-fast attacks gave him the upper hand. Jayavardhan watched in awe, amazed by Vatsalya's incredible speed and skill. He had never seen such a talented warrior before.

Soon, Vayuvraj' s sword lay on the ground, defeated by Vatsalya's extraordinary talent. The assembly was filled with admiration for Vatsalya's unmatched fighting skills. Jayavardhan finally understood why Muni Sahadri had chosen Vatsalya for this war. He was truly a master of his craft.

Prasiddha was the second warrior to enter the fray, but he too was quickly defeated. Five warriors banded together to fight Vatsalya, but even their combined efforts were no match for him.

As the tension eased, Vatsalya addressed the group. "All of you are strong warriors. We fight for the establishment of truth, knowledge, love, compassion, and Dharma, for the establishment of Bharatvarsh," he declared. "We fight to bring Ram Rajya to our land. Our selfishness is for the nation, and Ketubhan's is for himself. One of our warriors can take on ten of theirs. We will triumph in this war, even with a smaller army."

Vatsalya's words inspired new hope and enthusiasm in everyone present. They praised his skill and hailed him as their commander. Vaidehi saw a different side of Vatsalya, a fierce warrior beneath his calm exterior. Everyone was convinced that only Vatsalya could bring an end to the Sakayu dynasty and usher in a new era.

9. The Battle for Prasthapur

As everyone returned to the Pratipur Raj Bhavan, Vatsalya's heart swelled with determination for the impending battle. A formidable committee of warriors had been assembled, consisting of Vayuvraj, the fierce fighter, Rahisang, the strategic mastermind, Sanayu, the skilled warrior, and Vaidehi, the fearless fighter. The army was divided into five units, each led by highly skilled fighters and comprising 2,000 warriors. Half of the squad in each unit rode on horseback, while a third were skilled archers and the remaining warriors were adept at sword fighting. Vaidehi and Vatsalya tirelessly strategized, with a focus on manufacturing weapons in preparation for the war.

"Your energy and enthusiasm are commendable. I am honored to fight by your side in this battle," Vaidehi remarked to Vatsalya. ".

Vatsalya replied, " It's because of you that I'm inspired to lead this battle."

Vaidehi laughed, but her eyes locked onto Vatsalya's, causing her to feel both lost and uneasy. Nevertheless, with Vatsalya at the helm and the troops prepared for battle, they were ready to face any challenge that came their way.

Meanwhile, Ketubhan had never fathomed the possibility of war, living a life of luxury and comfort. His commander Mridant was equally negligent, preoccupied with indulging in the lavish royal lifestyle and shirking his responsibilities. Vatsalya's strategy was to attack the Prasthapur Raj Bhavan and defeat Ketubhan on his own turf.

As they made their way to Prasthapur, Vatsalya's army was divided into five predetermined units, with Vaidehi and Vatsalya leading one unit and Vayuvraj leading another.

Ketubhan, confident and unafraid, remained ignorant of the impending attack. But soon enough, Vatsalya's army arrived at Prasthapur, quickly surrounding the Raj Bhavan from all directions, with no escape routes left for Ketubhan. As word of the war spread, Commander Mridant sounded the battle cry, but the army inside the palace was unprepared and in disarray, unable to organize themselves in time. Meanwhile, Ketubhan emerged from his chambers, only to be met with the news of the surprise attack.

Ketubhan, in anger, said, "Which state has made this move? I will give everyone the punishment of death." Mridant replied, "My King, this situation will be brought under control very soon."

The soldiers of Ketubhan marched out of the palace for war. The army of Vatsalya was organized according to a strategic policy of warfare. Upon their arrival, Ketubhan's soldiers were showered with countless arrows, causing many casualties. In the chaos, the soldiers began to flee in different directions. Ketubhan's army was vast, but they were currently struggling under the heavy tactics of Vatsalya's warfare policy.

In the midst of a fierce battle, Commander Mridant's army was suddenly ambushed from the south, resulting in heavy casualties. However, the commander rallied his troops and engaged in direct combat. The clash of swords sent sparks flying, igniting the air with a fiery intensity as soldiers fought with everything they had. Blood spilled on the battlefield as the two armies engaged in a brutal struggle.

Commander Mridant's army fought only to defend themselves, but the army of Vatsalya fought for the whole of Bharatvarsh, their passion and strength evident in their attacks. One soldier from Vatsalya was able to take down ten enemy soldiers, and Vatsalya, Vayuvraj, and Vaidehi were able to defeat many of Ketubhan's warriors.

The two armies clashed, and Vatsalya faced off against Commander Mridant himself. Vatsalya's attacks were so powerful that they pushed Mridant's horse back. Mridant was thrown off his horse and Vatsalya charged towards him. Mridant's sword could not even touch Vatsalya due to his agility and ferocity. Ketubhan's best warrior started to feel hopeless. In front of Vatsalya, he looked like a child, and he was quickly defeated.

Ketubhan's army was surrounded, and death was inevitable. Ketubhan, who was once proud of his army, now saw them fall all around him. Ketubhan's two sons also met their end at the hands of Vatsalya. He too, now disheartened, took his sword and came forward for battle against Vatsalya, but Vatsalya killed him in just a few strokes.

After the death of Ketubhan, his soldiers knelt down. Ketubhan's young son Chandrabhan, who was only five years old, saw Vatsalya tear apart his father and brothers, but he could do nothing except shed tears. Ketubhan's wife Anasuya was successful in escaping with her son Chandrabhan through a secret route.

Vatsalya achieved victory in this battle, despite having an army ten times smaller than Ketubhan's vast army, he forced them to kneel down. Everyone began to congratulate Vatsalya. The news of Vatsalya's victory spread throughout Bharatvarsh faster than fire. Many kings in different states began to fear the name Vatsalya. The people were happy to see the end of the cruel dynasty, but they felt that another king had come to power through the strength of his army, and they did not have high hopes for the welfare of the people from Vatsalya.

10 . The Coronation of Rajan Vikramaditya: A New Era of Bharatvarsh

The news of victory filled the hearts of Muni Sahadri and king Jayavardhan with boundless joy. They set out from Pratipur towards Prasthapur, and upon arrival, they applauded all the warriors on this victory. Following this, an invitation was extended to the rulers of all the states in Bharatvarsh, knowledgeable sages, important members of society, farmers, and traders to come to Prasthapur. In just a few days, everyone had gathered. Hundreds of thousands of people attended this gathering. On one side of the assembly were sages and respected members of society, farmers and merchants sat on another side, and even kings were seated. The entire audience was captivated by Vatsalya's achievement, and they were astounded that he had conquered the enormous army of the Sakayu dynasty.

When everyone had calmed down, Muni Sahadri addressed the assembly and said, "Ketubhan oppressed the people and acted contrary to the values of Bharatvarsh. Shri Ram is the ideal king of Bharatvarsh, and every king of Bharatvarsh should follow his path. However, Ketubhan was behaving like a robber. This change of power was necessary and is in the best interest of all. Special thanks to King Jayavardhan for his assistance in making all of this possible."

The attendees congratulated King Jayavardhan, and he accepted the applause while standing.

After that, Muni Sahadri applauded Vatsalya, Vaidehi, Vayuvraj, and every warrior whose unmatched courage and bravery led to this victory. The entire assembly started clapping loudly in congratulation for everyone.

After the assembly fell silent, Muni Sahadri spoke up, "Bharatvarsh is in need of a new ruler, someone who can serve the people with selflessness, knowledge, bravery, and the ability to uphold the values of Bharatvarsh, and who can bring Ram Rajya even in the Kaliyuga. It is our good fortune that such a person is present among us, who is capable of bringing Ram Rajya. I propose the name of Vatsalya as the new ruler of Bharatvarsh to all of you."

Upon hearing this, the entire assembly stood up and congratulated Vatsalya. Vaidehi's eyes filled with tears, and even Jayavardhan joined in the applause. The celebration continued for some time, and eventually, the assembly quieted down, eagerly waiting for Vatsalya's address.

When everyone settled down, Vatsalya spoke, "Munivar! I did not fight this war with the intention of becoming a ruler. My goal was to restore the values and principles of Bharatvarsh. I believe that King Jayavardhan deserves the credit for this victory, and I propose that he be appointed as the new ruler of Bharatvarsh."

Muni Sahadri addressed Vatsalya with conviction, "King Jayavardhan and I firmly believe that you possess all the qualities that a ruler of Bharatvarsh should embody. Don't underestimate your potential, my son. You were born to fulfill this task. In the age of Kaliyuga, Bharatvarsh requires a ruler like you who can lead with compassion and wisdom."

Vaidehi supported Sahadri's proposal and added, "I agree with Munivar. Vatsalya is highly capable and fit for this position. Other people present in gathering also supported his appointment, and after considering everyone's opinion, Vatsalya humbly accepted this position with a spirit of service."

With the unanimous support of the assembly, Vatsalya was seated on the throne, and his coronation ceremony was conducted. He took an oath of serving the nation with utmost sincerity and devotion.

After this, Muni Sahadri said, "From today onwards, you will be known as 'Rajan Vikramaditya'. You do not belong to any royal dynasty, your duty is to serve this land that spreads between the Himalayas and the oceans; hence this dynasty will be known as Himsagar dynasty. Everyone congratulated him and thus the Himsagar dynasty was established and Vikramaditya became the ruler of Bharatvarsh."

The ascension of Vikramaditya, a ruler from a common tribe, marked a significant turning point in the history of Bharatvarsh. His humble background instilled a sense of connection and trust among the people. Meanwhile, Kaliyuga was witnessing this change of power. Ketubhan was ruling according to his wishes, but he was unaware of the impact this change of power would have on him.

Rajan Vikramaditya took the reins of power in Bharatvarsh immediately and effectively. He appointed Vayuvraj as the General. Muni Sahadri became his special advisor at the request of Vikramaditya. Vaidehi was made the Mahamantri, which was a post after the king. There were many challenges before the king. Vikramaditya and Vaidehi first decided to quickly resolve the issues of farmers and found a solution in a few days. They immediately ended the zamindari system and made the farmers the owners of the land. They also decided to buy their produce at fair prices.

This decision was historic in the history of Bharatvarsh. When the farmers heard this news, they could not believe it at first, but Vikramaditya and Vaidehi together implemented this decision at the grassroot level and turned it into reality. Tears flowed from the eyes of the farmers. Vikramaditya and Vaidehi themselves experienced the joy of the farmers. The farming community had been looted until now, but today they received the right to live with dignity.

After that, many states which were looting the people during the reign of the Sakayu dynasty, underwent a change of power. They relinquished power without war, fearing Vikramaditya.

Vikramaditya also established a separate institution for the justice system, which could punish him as well, according to the rules. Vikramaditya brought every decision for the welfare of the people to the ground level. He gave equal rights to transgender people. He made the decision to include them in the mainstream. They came to meet him and shared their pain, how they were discriminated against since birth, and how they were punished throughout their lives for a crime they didn't commit. Vikramaditya's eyes welled up with tears as he heard their story. He declared to them that in Bhartavarsh, the Ram Rajya cannot exist without giving equal rights to all of you. The King immediately provided them with a place to live in the main city and included their representatives in his assembly. They were given the right to education and employment.

Vikramaditya believed in karma and believed that no one's karma could be considered superior or inferior. No one could become anyone else's slave, and even the word "slave" was banned. Now, no class of society was ostracized.

Within a year, he set Bhartavarsh, on the path of Ram Rajya, and the people began to compare him to the ideal king of Bhartavarsh, Shri Ram.

Muni Sahadri was pleased with every decision of Vikramaditya. Vikramaditya never needed his special advice because he himself was not less knowledgeable than any wise sage.

(One day in the royal palace, during a conversation)

Muni Sahadri said, "King, you don't need me. You are knowledgeable and have foresight."

Vikramaditya replied, "Munivar, I cannot even imagine living in this palace without you. Seeing you reminds me of why you called me here."

Sahadri laughed and said, "Vikramaditya, you haven't changed yet."

To which Vikramaditya responded, "Munivar! Bharatvarsha is the wealthiest country in the world. But its real wealth is its knowledge. In this era of Kaliyuga, it is essential that this knowledge be gathered in one place. We should have a great university where this knowledge is easily accessible to everyone."

Sahadri praised Vikramaditya's idea, saying, "Your vision is excellent and extremely necessary in this Kaliyuga era. Bharatvarsh possesses the knowledge acquired through the penance of sages over thousands of years. However, this knowledge is scattered, and it is essential that we bring it together in one place through a university. With time, this knowledge will become even richer as the pursuit of knowledge is a continuous process. For human understanding, we have the Gita; for ideal behavior of a society, we have the Ramayana; for knowing the difference between right and wrong, we have the Mahabharata; for health, we have Ayurveda, and also the rare knowledge of yoga and so many different schools of philosophy. We also have astronomy to calculate time by knowing the position of stars and planets, and mathematics to make life easier. Gathering all this in one place will be extremely beneficial."

Vikramaditya informed Vaidehi about this proposal, and the next day, the proposal was discussed in the royal court and passed with unanimous consent. Thus, the first university of Bhartavarsh, Taxila, was established. It was constructed on the western coast of Bhartavarsh, along with the Hind Mahasagar. The building was even more spacious than the palace in Prasthapur where arrangements were made for teachers and students to stay. The building was white in color, and even the waves of the ocean paid homage to it. Knowledgeable individuals in every subject became Acharya here and started sharing knowledge, and learners began to acquire knowledge and become proficient. After the establishment of the university, Muni Sahadri also left the palace in Prasthapur and became the chief Acharya of Taxila. Vikramaditya also felt that Bhartavarsh needed Muni Sahadri at Taxila.

11. The Fall of a Mahamantri: A Tale of Love

After two years since his appointment, Rajan Vikramaditya made a decision to visit his ancestral tribe, Sinhdham. He extended an invitation to Vaidehi to join him on this journey, which she eagerly accepted. The prospect of seeing the place where Vikramaditya spent his childhood and youth filled Vaidehi with excitement, and she also planned to confess her love during the arduous journey. However, she couldn't ignore the nagging feeling of fear and uncertainty in her heart, like crossing a river of fire.

Lost in the midst of my journey,
I catch a glimpse of my destination,
A place that was once beyond my imagination.
What was distant from our eyes until yesterday,
Today it has started to show itself.
The clock ticks and time flies by,
My heart races and I hear my breath sigh.
This is the turning point, a crucial time in my life,
Where I must pass the test and face my strife.
But the path ahead is far from easy,
As doubts and fears make me feel queasy.
The mirror reflects my dwindling faith,
And I must find the courage to stay on this race.
I yearn for a life beyond the fire,
But crossing the river of flames will test my desire.

Vaidehi's heart was brimming with excitement as she embarked on this journey. She adorned herself in the most exquisite attire, with her rosy cheeks, straight hair, and adorned bosom complemented by the glint of gold and silver jewelry. After a few days of travel, Vikramaditya reached his tribe in Sinhdham.

The news of his arrival filled the people of the tribe with great joy, and the whole tribe was adorned with fragrant flowers. Vikramaditya, riding on a white horse with his army convoy, was welcomed with warm hugs and cheers from the tribe's people. The people of the tribe were ecstatic that Vikramaditya had become the king, but they still remembered him as Vatsalya, one amongst them. Tethavat's eyes were filled with tears of pride and joy as one of their own had ascended to become the king of Bharatvarsh.

Vaidehi was awestruck by the energy and beauty of the tribe, while Sugandha observed the scene from afar with great delight. Finally, Vikramaditya met with Sugandha and embraced her, causing Vaidehi's attention to shift entirely to them and momentarily eclipsing the beauty of the tribe from her mind. Both gazed silently into each other's eyes, and Sugandha understood Vaidehi's love for Vikramaditya, which was still unknown to him.

Afterwards, Vikramaditya introduced the two to each other, then, he introduced Vaidehi to all the people in the tribe. As he spoke of her bravery and heroism, Vikramaditya felt immensely proud. Sugandha, on the other hand, felt a pang of jealousy upon hearing Vikramaditya's praise of Vaidehi. Meanwhile, Vaidehi became consumed with worry, contemplating the nature of the bond between Sugandha and Vikramaditya.

At night, Sugandha and Vikramaditya set out for a stroll under the moonlight, while Vaidehi watched the scene from her guest chamber, unable to intervene.

They found themselves at the banks of the Stuti River, a place where they used to rendezvous often. With a sigh, Sugandha turned to Vikramaditya and spoke, "You speak highly of Vaidehi. I had a feeling that you would forget me and it seems that I was right. You are now a King and have Vaidehi by your side. I have no claim over you anymore."

Vikramaditya smiled and replied, " Let go of jealousy, Sugandha, My love for you remains unwavering. Vaidehi is the Mahamantri of Bharatvarsh and the kingdom needs her. That is why she is by my side."

Sugandha, her anger boiling over, retorted, "I find that hard to believe. You are a King, after all. You can do whatever you wish."

Vikramaditya responded calmly, "I am still the same Vatsalya you fell in love with. The title of King is merely a responsibility."

Suddenly, Vikramaditya got down on one knee and proposed to Sugandha. Overwhelmed, Sugandha couldn't contain her emotions any longer and threw her arms around Vikramaditya while crying. Thc couple announced their decision to the entire tribe, who had been eagerly waiting for this announcement. Everyone congratulated them on their impending nuptials, Vaidehi also heard this news.

I came to confess my emotions with innocence.
To make him mine, my heart took the chance,
For births, our love was to be true,
I yearned for it to be with only you.
But alas, fate had another plan,
And love slipped away from my hand.
True love found a home in someone else's heart,

Leaving me with a sense of rejection, tearing me apart.

The realization hit me like a tide,

My love, though true, was left unrequited.

Vaidehi's heart shattered into a million pieces as she learned of Vikramaditya's love for another. She put on a brave face and congratulated the happy couple, but her tears fell like raindrops in the solitude of her room that night. The following day, Vikramaditya and Sugandha were wed in a simple ceremony, and Vikramaditya returned to Prasthapur palace with his wife Sugandha.

With solemn simplicity, the union of Vikramaditya and Sugandha was consummated, leaving Vaidehi's heart in shards, Sugandha ascended to the throne as the new Queen of Bharatvarsh. Vaidehi struggled to forget the man who had captured her heart. She was unaware of Vikramaditya's feelings for another, and her love for him burned like a fire within her. Though she longed to confess her feelings, she remained silent, trapped in the prison of unrequited love.

As Vikramaditya and Sugandha basked in the glow of their love, Vaidehi cried alone in her room, unable to escape the memories of what could have been. Time passed, and Sugandha gave birth to a son who was named Mahendra, but Vaidehi's heart remained heavy with the weight of lost love.

As the royal court carried on with its daily proceedings, Vaidehi graced the court with her presence. Despite her efforts to conceal it, Sugandha could see the love in Vaidehi's eyes for the King Vikramaditya. This realization made Sugandha feel insecure and envious of Vaidehi's beauty and charm. In an attempt to compete with her,

Sugandha started to lavish more attention on her own appearance. She even went so far as to converse with Vaidehi with disdain, hoping to intimidate her rival. Despite Sugandha's contemptuous behavior, Vaidehi never lost her cool. She understood that Sugandha's feelings stemmed from jealousy and didn't want to jeopardize Vikramaditya's personal life by letting their differences get in the way. Vaidehi knew that true love meant putting the other person's happiness above one's own desires. Hence, after much contemplation, Vaidehi made the difficult decision to resign from her prestigious position as the Mahamantri.

Five years after Vikramaditya became king, Vaidehi made the decision to resign from her position as Mahamantri. She went to his chamber to inform him of her decision. That day, Vikramaditya was alone in his chamber. He welcomed Vaidehi with a smile.

"King! I want to talk about a very important matter," Vaidehi said, trying to hide her pain of love.

"You addressed me as King for the first time," Vikramaditya responded, noticing the change.

Vaidehi remained silent.

"What is it that you want to talk about?" Vikramaditya inquired.

"I want to return to my kingdom Pratipur," Vaidehi said.

"Why?" Vikramaditya asked, sounding distraught.

"My duty here is done, and I am tired," Vaidehi replied, her voice laced with sadness.

Standing in his place, Vikramaditya approached Vaidehi and said, "We fought for the values of Bharatvarsh, and I am incomplete without you. My story is incomplete without you, Vaidehi. Bringing Ram Rajya to Bharatvarsha is as much your responsibility as it is mine. You cannot abandon me in this condition. Today, if Bharatvarsh is progressing towards Ram Rajya, then the biggest reason for it is you, Vaidehi. Muni Sahadri have already left. I cannot rule without you. If you want to become a King, then I will appoint you and return to my tribe."

Vaidehi, crying, said, "Do you think I want to become King?" Without thinking, she hugged Vikramaditya while crying. She felt a peace she had never experienced in her entire life. With her eyes closed, she was lost in Vikramaditya's embrace when suddenly Sugandha entered the room. Seeing this scene, she became angry and pushed Vaidehi away and slapped her hard, saying, "Shameless woman! Your lust is not fulfilled at night, that during the day you cling to someone else's husband like a serpent. And this characterless woman is the Mahamantri of Bharatvarsh. For so many years, your heart has not been filled with Vikramaditya. Now go find another man. "

Vikramaditya could not understand anything. He did not even feel anger. But upon hearing these words for Vaidehi, tears welled up in his eyes. Sugandha counseled Vikramaditya on the path of an ideal king. Vikramaditya had never looked at Vaidehi from the perspective that Sugandha was thinking. The love between them was selfless, and that too, only from Vaidehi's side. Vaidehi started crying uncontrollably and left feeling guilty. She felt that she had committed a grave sin. Vikramaditya couldn't even say a word to stop her.

As the sun rose on a new day, Vaidehi had already left the palace. It was a joyous day for Sugandha.

Vikramaditya arrived at the royal court as usual. He didn't discuss the events of the previous day with anyone. He concealed his emotions and informed the entire assembly of Vaidehi's sudden decision to return to Pratipur.

Vayuvraj said, "But, King when will the Mahamantri return."

Vikramaditya responded, "You know that the king of Pratipur, Jayavardhan, is now elderly and needs Vaidehi's presence more than ever. We should honor her decision."

Vayuvraj argued, "But Vaidehi is the most important pillar of this assembly, and her responsibility towards Bharatvarsh is even greater than that towards her own family."

Vikramaditya replied, "Undoubtedly, but for now we need to bring the dream of Ram Rajya to fruition in Bharatvarsh with the same vigour, even without her."

Vayuvraj was disappointed with Vaidehi's decision. He urged Vikramaditya to persuade her to return after a few days, but Vikramaditya did not give a positive response. After this, Vayuvraj remained silent and did not attempt to learn more.

After Sugandha humiliated Vaidehi, Vikramaditya couldn't muster the courage to stop Vaidehi from leaving. He held Vaidehi in high regard and began to see himself as responsible for her insolence. He couldn't separate himself from Sugandha, and he couldn't bring Vaidehi back to the palace. Vikramaditya was now alone. However, his determination didn't waver. He improved the governance system even further and dedicated his time to serving his people. After Vaidehi's devastating humiliation, Vikramaditya's relationship with Sugandha crumbled. He couldn't bear to spend even a single night with her, his love for her withered away, and he stopped talking to her altogether.

Meanwhile, Sugandha basked in the glory of being Queen of Bharatvarsh, but her heart was filled with anger towards Vikramaditya. She had no interest or inclination towards Vikramaditya's commitment to bringing Ram Rajya to Bharatvarsh. She instigated her son Mahendra against Vikramaditya. She blamed Vikramaditya's love for Vaidehi for their misfortune. Even her love for Vikramaditya had dwindled, and now she waited for Mahendra to take his rightful place on the throne. Vikramaditya was an ideal for the whole of Bharatvarsha, but he was no longer an ideal for his own son.

Vikramaditya remained unaware of these developments. He still considered the throne as a responsibility and a means of service. Muni Sahadri and Vaidehi had left his side, and he was alone. However, his desire to bring Ram Rajya to fruition did not diminish. He devoted every moment to realizing this dream. Under Vikramaditya's reign, Bhartavarsh reached new heights. No one in his kingdom was unhappy. He visited Taxila several times to discuss his new decisions with Muni Sahadri.

Vaidehi had now begun living in Pratipur. She found it increasingly challenging to carry on without Vikramaditya by her side. She was also disengaged from the affairs of the Pratipur kingdom. She could not even confide in anyone about her true feelings for Vikramaditya, knowing that her love for him had now become the source of her anguish. She was in such agony for which there seemed to be no remedy.

One day, king Jayavardhan summoned Vaidehi to his chamber. Vaidehi entered concealing her turmoil. Commending Vikramaditya, Jayavardhan said, "We must have accrued good karma in our past lives to be able to assist him. Comparisons are now being drawn between him and Shri Ram due to his endeavors to end the Kaliyuga."

Then, placing his hand on Vaidehi's head, he said, "Daughter! You played a momentous role in Vikramaditya's triumph."

Vaidehi replied, "He is capable himself. It is the good fortune of the entire Bharatvarsh that he is our king."

After this, Jayavardhan coughed, and Vaidehi promptly gave him water from a nearby vessel. After a short pause, he said, "Daughter! My last wish is to see your marriage. You have fulfilled your responsibility and come back, and now is the appropriate time for marriage." Vaidehi instantly replied, "I don't think I should get married."

The king said, "No, daughter. Not getting married goes against our tradition. Even after marriage, you will still be the heiress of my kingdom. Don't refuse my final wish."

Vaidehi became calm. She knew that she would never be able to have Vikramaditya in this life. So, upon her father's repeated request, she agreed to get married. King Jayavardhan was pleased with Vaidehi's decision.

King Jayavardhan embarked on a quest to find the perfect groom for his beloved daughter Vaidehi, and after a long search, he finally found Prince Subahu of Tryambapur to be a worthy match. With great enthusiasm, he proposed the union to his dear friend King Manik of Tryambapur, who eagerly accepted the proposal without hesitation. Subahu also felt fortunate to have a bride like Vaidehi, who was not only beautiful, but also brave and intelligent. For Vaidehi, Vikramaditya was the only suitable suitor in the entire Bharatvarsh, but now she too, forgetting her love, had made the decision to marry Subahu. The grand wedding ceremony was conducted soon after, filled with splendor, music, and dance, as Vaidehi bid farewell to her old life and moved to Tryambapur.

Vaidehi was unfamiliar to Subahu, but he had heard from somewhere that she had spent many years with Vikramaditya. On the first night of their marriage, Subahu was engrossed in heavy drinking with his friends when Chirahu remarked, 'Prince, tonight is your first night with Princess Vaidehi, but I have heard that she has spent many years alone with Vikramaditya. This will not be her first night. "

(Laughter erupted from everyone)

Subahu overheard it all and promptly chimed in, "It is also true that there is no fairy more beautiful than her in the whole world." Saying this, he choked on the drink of intoxication.

Having an apsara like Vaidehi as his wife, Subahu became arrogant, and Vaidehi's luscious bosoms, wide thighs, pink lips, and enchanting waist began to increase his lust. Driven by his lusty desire and intoxication, he barged into her chamber with the intention of taking advantage of Vaidehi while she was lying on the bed.

"He came close and touched her. It was the first time Vaidehi had been touched by a man and that too against her will. She was shaken and thoughts of Vikramaditya flooded her mind. Her love for Vikramaditya now thwarted her from giving her body to anyone else. Never did Vaidehi think at the time of her marriage that she would be unable to give herself to another man. She pushed Subahu away and stood tall. Subahu's anger flared up, and he attempted to overpower her with his strength. He started tearing off Vaidehi's clothes in a violent frenzy. Despite Vaidehi's screams, Subahu was consumed by his insatiable lust and desire. He fervently kissed her breasts and tenderly caressed his body against hers to satisfy his overwhelming carnal urges "I will keep you like a slave and do this to you every day," said Subahu, kissing Vaidehi. But Vaidehi was a warrior. The warrior within her awakened. She pushed Subahu away again and he fell. Without hesitation, she grabbed a nearby vessel and struck him forcefully on the head, rendering him unconscious. Vaidehi fled from there."

Vaidehi ran towards the city of Pratipur, breaking through the massive walls of the royal palace. Her heart was pounding, and due to the swift pace of her run, her breath started to quicken. As she ran, a realization hit her: she no longer held any claim to Pratipur. Her father's name had already been disgraced, and there was no advantage in returning there. Suddenly, she stopped in her tracks, calling out Vikramaditya's name with a mixture of tears and laughter, vowing that they would be reunited and started running toward north. But as she continued her path, thoughts of Sugandha's cruel actions flooded her mind, causing her to come to a halt once again. She could not go to Prasthapur, either. So she sank down, clad in her bridal garments, and wept under the starry sky, gazing up at the moon with a heavy heart.

She found no way and now proceeded to walk towards the Southern Ocean. Moving at a fast pace while crying, she reached the shore of the vast ocean where she intended to give up her life. She, who played an important role in the victory of a great warrior, Vikramaditya, and was his Mahamantri, was now going to end her life in this way. She stopped for a moment in front of the ocean and threw her jewelry there. Is she indecent? Does the whole Bharatvarsh think about her this way?

She advanced towards the ocean, her body began sinking in the water, and her tears began to merge with the ocean. When the water reached her nose, suddenly a voice came from behind - "Stop!" She turned back and saw a yogi with a glow. His face was not clearly visible. He said - "You cannot surrender to death in such cowardice."

Vaidehi stood there, gazing in awe as the yogi said. "Practice to attain what you desire. In your next birth, you will have it. You are a great warrior of Bharatvarsh who did not receive the honor she deserved. Practice, young woman," he advised before disappearing into the ether.

Vaidehi remained transfixed for some time before finally coming to her senses. The yogi had already vanished into thin air. Vaidehi then settled down on the shore and began practicing yoga to calm her mind and felt grateful for the experience of love with Vikramaditya. She realized that King Jayavardhan was a great father. She began to feel happy again, but not being able to have true love was causing her a lot of pain. Once again, tears started flowing down her cheeks, but she was now calm. She had control over her breath. She sat there practicing for some time, and then headed towards the northeastern Himalayas.

Next day upon learning of the incident, king Jayavardhan was filled with dismay. The state Tryambapur posed a threat to Pratipur. Vikramaditya was informed of the situation by Jayavardhan. Without delay, Vikramaditya arrived in Pratipur and inquired about Vaidehi. However, Jayavardhan, unable to answer, was in a state of uncontrollable tears. After investigating with Subahu and Tryambapur, it was discovered that a young woman dressed in bridal attire had gone towards the ocean a few days prior. Upon reaching the shore, Vaidehi's jewelry was found. King Jayavardhan believed that Vaidehi had taken her own life and began to cry loudly. Vikramaditya also believed this to be the case, and they could only mourn Vaidehi's passing with tears.

Vikramaditya experienced a pain that he had never felt before. However, he still didn't say anything. He did not take any action against Subahu. He did not even attempt to find out why Vaidehi took such a step on the first night of her marriage. He did not want to accept his love for Vaidehi. However, he began to consider himself guilty for Vaidehi's suicide. Even Muni Sahadri received this sad news, but he could not do anything beyond shedding tears.

12. The Journey of Chandrabhan: Conquering the Mind and Fulfilling Destiny

Amidst the battle between Vikramaditya and Ketubhan, Chandrabhan and Anasuya had to flee for their lives. They sought refuge with the Khandava tribe, deep in a forest miles away from their home. Chandrabhan was haunted by the memories of the bloody scene of Vikramaditya killing his father and brothers with his sword. After spending few days in this tribe, Anasuya sought help from Ketubhan's friends, but they were all too self-centred to lend a hand. No one came to their aide. Anasuya was left completely alone. She was turned away from every door. Her self-respect was shattered in every place. Chandrabhan witnessed it all, deeply sensing her pain. He held Vikramaditya solely responsible for his predicament, harboring deep resentment towards him, and his desire for revenge intensified.

Alone and rejected, the two became victims of poverty, struggling to survive day by day. One day, hungry and desperate, they stumbled upon the banks of the Sangya River. Amidst the barren landscape, Chandrabhan spotted a mango tree and quickly climbed it, plucking the fruit and dropping it down for his mother. Despite being raw and unripe, the mangoes tasted like the sweetest delicacies to their starving stomachs.

Chandrabhan and Anasuya sat under the mango tree, feeling the satisfaction of their hunger. Chandrabhan, filled with determination, made a bold statement to his mother -

"Maa, we don't need anyone's help. We will do this on our own."

Anasuya, with a reassuring hand on his head, spoke wise words - "Where friendship is built on selfishness, it always crumbles. Even your father was blinded by it. Don't let that become you."

Emboldened by his mother's words, Chandrabhan proclaimed his goal, "I want to become the King of Bharatvarsh and bring Vikramaditya to his knees."

Anasuya's eyes gleamed with pride and conviction as she spoke, "You will be the King of Bharatvarsh. You will overthrow Vikramaditya and take his place."

After this, Anasuya and Chandrabhan took refuge in a tribe near the Sangya shore without revealing their true identity and began living a simple life, but they both had grand ambitions. Despite the people's love for Vikramaditya's leadership, Chandrabhan couldn't help but feel envious and resentful towards him. Anasuya noticed this and decided to advise him with affection.

"Son," she said, "don't let your desire to become a King be consumed by revenge. Instead of being jealous of Vikramaditya, learn from him. If he rose from humble beginnings to become a king, then you can do it too. In the struggle for power, war and death are commonplace. You need to become stronger than him and win back your kingdom that he has usurped. Everyone loves Vikramaditya, so you should strive to become a king who is equally adored by the people. To do so, you must surpass Vikramaditya in power in every aspect and overthrow him from his throne."

Chandrabhan's mind became resolute on this notion. The smouldering flames of retribution were consuming him from within. He comprehended the arduousness of his journey and thus commenced an inquiry into Vikramaditya, shelving his vindictive sentiments. Chandrabhan was consumed by his desire to become a great warrior like Vikramaditya. He spent years learning about him, listening to his stories, and attending his public gatherings. He developed admiration for Vikramaditya, Chandrabhan's goal was to defeat him and become the king himself.

But he couldn't understand how Vikramaditya had become such a powerful warrior despite his humble beginnings. Determined to find out, Chandrabhan journeyed to the Sinhdham tribe where he discovered the secret of Vikramaditya's strength. It turned out that the great warrior had spent three years alone in the snow-capped mountains of the Himalayas, honing his skills and becoming unbeatable. Chandrabhan realized that Vikramaditya's strength lay in his deep understanding of himself, which he attributed to the teachings of the Gita.

Chandrabhan yearned to follow in the footsteps of the legendary Vikramaditya, and his heart burned with a fierce desire to become the ruler of Bharatvarsh. When he shared his aspirations with his mother Anasuya, she beamed with pride and promised to support him in his quest. "My dear son," she said, "if you wish to discover your true self through the path of renunciation, then I am with you every step of the way. Always remember, Your only goal in life is to dethrone Vikramaditya and become the ruler of Bharatvarsh."

Eager to fulfil his mother's prophecy and claim his rightful place as the King, Chandrabhan vowed to dethrone Vikramaditya. "Once I become the King," he proclaimed, "I will take you with all the honour and respect you deserve to the grand Raj Bhavan in Prasthapur."

Blessed by his mother's loving encouragement, Chandrabhan set out on his journey the very next day. Armed with the sacred Gita and his trusty sword, he made his way into the heart of the Himalayan wilderness, where no mortal had dared to venture before.

The forest was shrouded in a thick veil of darkness, and even the moon's rays could not penetrate the dense canopy of trees. As the growls of wild beasts echoed through the stillness of the night, Chandrabhan's heart began to pound with fear. Desperate to protect himself, he scrambled up a nearby tree and drew his trusty sword. Tears streamed down his face as he gazed out into the impenetrable gloom.

At just fifteen years old, Chandrabhan's quest to emulate Vikramaditya had led him to this treacherous place. The night passed, and the rays of the sun woke him up the next day, he couldn't go back. He controlled his fear and first ate fruit to calm his hunger, and then after wandering around for a while, he found a cave where he could spend the night. He also arranged for a fire and slept without any worry that night. He felt it was a great achievement. He studied the teachings of the Gita with a fervent devotion and honed his skills as a hunter with every passing day. And as the seasons changed and the months slipped by, he slowly began to acclimate to the harsh realities of life in the forest.

But even as he adapted to his new surroundings, Chandrabhan remained haunted by the question that weighed heavily on his mind - how would he ever achieve his goal in this remote and forbidding place?

One day, As the rain poured down in a symphony of sweet melody, Chandrabhan climbed towards the towering peak of the Himalayan range. And there, through the mist and the rain, he caught a glimpse of a sacred ashram nestled amidst the clouds.

Filled with excitement, he rushed towards the entrance of the Ashram, eager to explore this mysterious new world. But as he stepped forward, a voice called out from within - "Stop! Do not enter."

Chandrabhan froze in his tracks as a wise old sage emerged from the shadows. His flowing white robes and long white beard spoke of a life dedicated to the pursuit of divine wisdom.

"My son," the sage spoke, "I have forsaken the temptations of the world and seek only the path of the divine. I have no desire to meet with any mortal. You must turn back now."

Chandrabhan's heart sank at these words. It had been a year since he had last laid eyes on another human being, and the prospect of a chance encounter had filled him with hope and excitement.

With folded hands, he called out to the revered sage, pleading for refuge from the storm. "Munivar," he implored, "Please grant me entry and offer me shelter from this tempestuous downpour."

“I don’t think even deluge can harm you”, said sage.

Despite the sage's initial reluctance, Chandrabhan did not give up. The next day, he returned to the ashram once again, this time with a copy of the Gita in his hands. But once again, the sage barred his entry, stating that he had no desire to engage with the outside world.

Undeterred, Chandrabhan continued to visit the ashram day after day, carrying the sacred text with him each time. Though he was refused entry each time, he refused to be discouraged.

For three long months, Chandrabhan persisted in his quest for knowledge. Day after day, he would come to the entrance of the ashram and silently read from the Gita.

After three months, upon seeing Chandrabhan's dedication towards knowledge, the sage invited him to the ashram.

Chandrabhan entered the ashram with trepidation, but upon stepping inside, he felt a surge of positive energy. He started looking around the ashram with enthusiasm, taking in every corner of it.

The wise sage gazed upon Chandrabhan and spoke, "Ketubhan's son, what brings you in Himalayas?"

Chandrabhan, sensing the sage's immense power, mustered his courage and revealed his true intentions. "I seek to tap into my full potential, to dethrone Vikramaditya and to become the King of Bharatvarsh. I have been following in the footsteps of Vikramaditya, but I am yet to find my way. Only you can guide me, make me your disciple, and show me the path."

A faint smile crept across the sage's lips, and he chuckled. "I am Muni Samved, and I do not take disciples. But your willpower and dedication impress me. I shall adopt you as my disciple.

Sage posed the question, "After a year of wandering in the forest and studying the sacred Gita, what have you learned?"

Chandrabhan was only sixteen years old. Upon being asked this question by the sage, he became calm. Then the sage said again, "Tell me which verse you liked the best."

Chandrabhan was hesitant at first, but he eventually replied, "Prabhu Sri Krishna said that for the one who has conquered the mind, the mind is the greatest friend, but for the one who has not been able to do so, the mind will remain the biggest enemy. And for the person who has conquered the mind, there is no difference between pleasure and pain, cold and heat, honour and disgrace. That person can see both friend and enemy with equal compassion."

Muni Samved was impressed by Chandrabhan's response and remained silent for a moment, taking in the wisdom of Prabhu Sri Krishna's words. Chandrabhan continued, "Arjuna asked Prabhu Shri Krishna how to control the fickle, stubborn, and extremely powerful mind, which is even more difficult to control than the wind. Then Prabhu Shri Krishna said that although it is very difficult to control the fickle mind, it is possible with continuous practice."

Muni Samved then asked, "Chandrabhan, what have you learned from Prabhu Sri Krishna's teachings?" Chandrabhan paused before replying, "I have conquered my fear by triumphing over my mind. Fear used to make me doubtful about the success of any task, but now I have no doubts. I have also overcome anger and lust, which are the biggest enemies of human beings, and greed cannot thrive within me."

Muni Samved was curious and asked, "Have you achieved victory over desire as well?" Chandrabhan thought for a moment before answering, "I have only one desire, and that is to become the King of Bharatvarsh. This desire is not an enemy, but a friend. I have conquered my enemies - anger, lust, greed, and attachment."

Muni Samved chuckled and said, "Perhaps you are speaking the truth, but I still can't believe you. However, I have a soloution." He showed a vessel to Chandrabhan and said, "This vessel contains deadly poison. If you have truly conquered your mind, this poison will not harm you even a bit. But if your mind-conquering statement turns out to be wrong, you will die."

At the tender age of sixteen, Chandrabhan lived a solitary life as a sanyasi, bereft of any spiritual guidance from a guru for nearly a year. When Muni Samved posed a question to him, Chandrabhan responded with unabashed innocence and truthfulness, little realizing the complexity involved in comprehending oneself.

Driven by a desire to explore the depths of his being, Chandrabhan took a drastic step in haste, consuming deadly poison. The deadly poison he consumed ravaged his senses, traveling from his tongue to his throat and down to his stomach. Throughout this harrowing experience, Muni Samved looked on in complete silence.

With the poison coursing through his veins, Chandrabhan lost control of the vessel he held, releasing it from his grip. A cacophony of coughing ensued, accompanied by blood seeping from his ears and nose. As he lay dying on the ground, his face pressed to the earth, Chandrabhan remained oblivious to his own dire state. Lamentably, he was unable to articulate any words as he lay before Muni Samved in an utterly pitiable condition.

Muni Samved observed Chandrabhan's condition without flinching for a few moments. He closed his eyes and assumed a meditative pose, saying, "Chandrabhan! Focus your mind, my son! Focus. Bring your breath under control."

Chandrabhan did not wish to depart from this mortal realm without becoming a King of Bharatvarsh. He attempted to concentrate his mind, but it was not an easy task. Suddenly, Muni Samved spoke again, "Sit down and meditate, my child."

Chandrabhan did not wish to suffer such a fate, so he got up from his agonized position and began to meditate once more. However, the poison had already spread throughout his entire body, and blood was flowing from his eyes as well.

Muni Samved spoke in a high-pitched voice, "Focus, Chandrabhan. Concentrate on your breath, my son."

Chandrabhan made every effort to follow the instruction, but he could not succeed.

Then Muni Samved shouted again and said, "Chandrabhan! Don't waste your final moments. Control your mind. Abandon the fear of death." Now, Chandrabhan focused his mind and normalized his breathing, and after a while, the effect of poison started to diminish from his body. Chandrabhan became normal again and was saved from death. He joined his hands, feeling embarrassed, and said, "Munivar! I did not lie." Muni Samved replied, "I know. Understanding oneself completely is not easy. You have come a long way. I accept you as my disciple."

Chandrabhan spent the next ten years under the guidance of Muni Samved. He learned not only scripture, yoga but also the most difficult styles of warfare, which were known to only a few in Bharatvarsh. After a decade passed, Chandrabhan had become proficient in every subject.

Muni Samved said, "Chandrabhan, you can return to pursue your goal. Your *shiksha* is complete." Chandrabhan bowed before the Muni.

"However, you have one vice. Your desire for the position of King is very strong," Muni Samved said.

"My only goal is to become a King in place of Vikramaditya," Chandrabhan replied.

Muni Samved laughed, "You are not different from him. But he conquered his desire, and you do not want to."

Chandrabhan asked, "How do you know him?"

Muni replied, "He was also my disciple." Chandrabhan understood everything.

Muni chuckled, "There is one more difference. What you did in ten years, he did in three years."

Chandrabhan smiled and asked, "Why did you help me?"

Muni Samved replied, "I told you; you are no different from him." After this, Chandrabhan took permission from Muni Samved and returned to his tribe."

After a decade of rigorous training and study under the guidance of Muni Samved, Chandrabhan returned to his homeland to reunite with his mother, Anasuya. She was overwhelmed with joy at the sight of her son, who had transformed into a handsome, powerful figure with a magnetic aura. She embraced him, and Chandrabhan reassured her that he would soon become the King of Bharatvarsh, fulfilling her long-standing desire.

Anasuya expressed her unwavering faith in Chandrabhan's abilities and encouraged him to meet his uncle Vrijbhan, who had played a crucial role in making his father the King of Bharatvarsh, despite never accepting the position himself.

This was new to Chandrabhan, and he was eager to learn more about his uncle's legacy and the hidden history of his family's ascent to power. Chandrabhan did not waste any time and embarked on his journey.

As the sun rose high in the sky, Chandrabhan mounted his black steed and set off on his journey. He wore a rugged brown outfit, with a gleaming sword strapped to his back. His destination was Tisthapur, home to the legendary Vrijbhan, younger brother of the mighty Ketubhan.

Vrijbhan had been the driving force behind Ketubhan's ascent to the throne of Bharatvarsh, thanks to his cunning strategies and prowess on the battlefield. But the two brothers had ultimately parted ways over their differing visions for ruling the kingdom. Vrijbhan had renounced his position and retired to Tisthapur.

After the victory of Vikramaditya, Vrijbhan never showed interest in power again. However, he had not abandoned his love for weapons. He was counted among the greatest warriors of Bharatvarsh. Even Vikramaditya had offered him a role as a trainer, which he had refused.

Chandrabhan reached Tisthapur and asked the people to help him find Vrijbhan and finally reached at his dwelling.

When he saw Vrijbhan, he laughed and said, "Uncle! I am Chandrabhan, son of Ketubhan and Anasuya."

Vrijbhan was taken aback, Chandrabhan looked like his mother Anasuya, Vrijbhan was overjoyed at the sight of his long-lost nephew. Tears streamed down his face as he hugged Chandrabhan tightly. "Son, you're alive!"

After a warm welcome, Vrijbhan poured Chandrabhan a cup of *kahwa* and asked about his sister-in-law, Anasuya. "Has she forgotten me like your father?" he inquired.

Chandrabhan retorted immediately, "No, Uncle! She herself had sent me to you so that I may accelerate on the path to become King of Bharatvarsh."

Vrijbhan chuckled upon hearing this and replied, "Do not harbour delusions, Chandrabhan. The comparison with Vikramaditya is futile. He is an invincible warrior, his defeat an arduous task."

Chandrabhan persisted, "Uncle, now is our time. No one thought that Ketubhan could be vanquished, yet Vikramaditya succeeded by killing him and ascending the throne."

Vrijbhan asked, "Do you seek revenge?"

Chandrabhan replied, "Not revenge, I desire the throne. We will follow in the footsteps of Vikramaditya." Vrijbhan looked towards Chandrabhan and said, "You possess a completely serene personality, devoid of any agitation. You are filled with self-control and don't even know anger. Your father was not like you."

Chandrabhan interrupted, "Uncle, forget all that and let us focus our attention on the royal throne. We need a vast army and assistants in every state of Bharatvarsh." Vrijbhan thought for a moment and asked, "You are talking like a king, but are you capable of fighting a war to acquire the throne?" Chandrabhan confidently replied, "You are the greatest warrior of entire Bharatvarsh. Just the thought of fighting with you makes every warrior afraid, but I can defeat you."

Angered by this, Vrijbhan said, "Chandrabhan, stop talking and let's fight!" He then raised his sword and attacked Chandrabhan.

In the very first attack, Vrijbhan had pushed Chandrabhan back, but Chandrabhan quickly recovered. He drew his sword and began to strike Vrijbhan in return. Chandrabhan easily dodged Vrijbhan' s fatal blows. At first, he only defended himself, but then he started to launch aggressive strikes. His every attack was very intense, and his body balance did not falter in any of the strikes. Vrijbhan had never seen such a warrior before. Soon, Vrijbhan' s sword slipped from his hand due to Chandrabhan's fierce attacks, and now he started laughing with his sword around Vrijbhan' s neck. Vrijbhan also began to laugh at his defeat.

After that, both sat down calmly. Now Chandrabhan gave Vrijbhan a cup of *kahwa*. Taking a sip, Vrijbhan said, "Let's start from Mythpur. There lives Kashav who was our warrior. He has other warriors too. He hides in the jungle due to fear of Vikramaditya. He is full of revenge and can be of great use to us."

Chandrabhan chuckled, "Yes, We will only add fuel to the fire. Those who seek revenge against Vikramaditya without any selfish motives will assist us willingly."

So, after including Kashav in their plan in Mythpur, Vrijbhan and Chandrabhan started traveling across the country to form an army against Vikramaditya. They wanted to defeat Vikramaditya and regain their lost power. They began recruiting people who also sought revenge against Vikramaditya and wanted to regain their lost power because of him. Seeing Vrijbhan and Chandrabhan, they were confident that they could defeat Vikramaditya.

One day, on their journey, Vrijbhan and Chandrabhan were traveling on horseback to the north-eastern region of Bharatvarsh to meet Nilanka, who ruled over the region during the reign of Ketubhan. Looking towards Chandrabhan, Vrijbhan said, "Power cannot be obtained while Vikramaditya is alive. If he dies, we may have an opportunity."

Chandrabhan responded, "You are speaking the truth, Uncle".

Vrijbhan continued, "I have another fear. The people who will accompany us to gain power are selfish and greedy. We will not be able to provide proper governance to the people, and it is possible that you may also lose power like Ketubhan."

Chandrabhan said, "These people are only assisting us in gaining power. We will set the policies. My only aspiration is for that throne, I am not avaricious, nor am I a slave of lust. The people will receive just governance, but this issue will arise only once Vikramaditya is no longer in power.

13. The Turning of the Wheel of Time

Two decades had passed under the reign of Vikramaditya. Anger, Greed, Lust, and Attachment had begun to weaken during his rule. The power that they had acquired during the reign of Ketubhan was now diminishing, while Compassion, Love, and Austerity began to grow stronger.

In Manvantar Loka, Kaliyuga came to his court, and everyone stood up in respect for him. Despairingly, Anger spoke in the assembly, "Lord! We are all becoming weak after the arrival of Vikramaditya. Our control over humans is decreasing. This is not good for your conquest of the universe."

Lust added, "Your Majesty! It seems that with the arrival of Vikramaditya, time has turned on its axis. The reign of ideal King Shri Ram is coming back, and we are all becoming helpless."

Kaliyuga listened to everyone's words carefully. Then he spoke with a smile, "In my age, the dream of Ram Rajya is impossible. Only Shri Ram can bring it. Undoubtedly, Vikramaditya wants to bring the reign of ideal King Shri Ram and he is immersed in it that now he has started to see himself as Shri Ram. However, to become Shri Ram is not possible for any human being in my era. "

Attachment said, "What do you mean, We are not able to comprehend?"

Kaliyuga spoke, "Do not lose hope. Vikramaditya is weak. He has started to think of himself as Shri Ram and has become trapped under this illusion. The desire to become like Shri Ram will harm him."

Lust responded with a smile, "Your statement seems to be true, my Lord!"

Kaliyuga added, “Lust! Stay close to Vikramaditya's son Mahendra. He may become your slave at any time. Keep searching for such an opportunity and take advantage of it when the time comes."

Then Kaliyuga spoke further about making Attachment dominant over Vikramaditya.

Kaliyuga in serious noted said, "We all exist within humans. However, we must dominate them at the right time so that they remain entirely under our control."

(Everyone laughs)

Then Anger said, "But, there will always be someone or the other who will be an obstacle for us in Bharatvarsh." Kaliyuga replied, "Only for a short time."

Lust asked, "What do you mean?"

Kaliyuga said, "If we want to increase our influence throughout the universe, Bharatvarsh will have to be destroyed, and we will need a power outside Bharatvarsh that can destroy it."

Attachment said, "Leader! We do not understand your statement."

Kaliyuga replied, "The people of Bharatvarsh cannot rule their own nation. There should be a ruler from outside of this land who can prove their knowledge false, and this can only be possible when the ruler here is an outsider. This task will take time, but I will definitely do it."

Lust asked, "Is it really possible?" to which Kaliyuga replied, "In this yuga, everything is possible." Kaliyuga instructed everyone to continue working as per his orders. Attachment then said, "Master, I will now reside in

Vikramaditya. His temptation to compare himself with Shri Ram will harm him. At the appropriate time, I will dominate him." Everyone laughed and the meeting was concluded.

Meanwhile, Vikramaditya was still firmly following the rules of governance. The people compared him to Shri Ram, which pleased Vikramaditya greatly. Prabhu Shri Krishna said in the Gita, "A person should perform his duty constantly without being attached to the results, for by doing karma without attachment, one attains the Supreme." However, Vikramaditya had now begun to forget this knowledge and was giving an opportunity for Attachment to dominate him.

As the wheel of time turned, Vikramaditya established the old glory of Bharatvarsh once again. Taxila University became the greatest institution of learning in the land under Muni Sahadri. After heading this institution for decades, he had stepped down from his position and dedicated his time to spiritual practices only. Muni Sahadri was pleased with the appointment of Vikramaditya to the throne of Bharatvarsh. Due to Vikramaditya's reign, the impact of the Kaliyuga was diminishing. Vaidehi's contribution was also very important, but her departure saddened him greatly.

Mahendra, the son of Vikramaditya and Sugandha, had grown up to be a young man. From childhood, he was arrogant and stubborn, lacking both in knowledge acquisition and warrior skills. Mahendra considered claim to every treasure of the kingdom as his birthright.

After the humiliation of Vaidehi by Sugandha, Vikramaditya never spent time with Sugandha and Mahendra again. He remained busy with his duties towards the people.

He never knew what his son was doing or how he thought. Sugandha always supported Mahendra's behavior, and no one ever complained to Vikramaditya about his son's actions. Mahendra was the prince of Bharatvarsh, lost in his own self-indulgent activities, while Vikramaditya remained oblivious to it all.

14. Attachment and the Fall of a King: The Tragic Story of Vikramaditya

Prince Mahendra lived a life of pure indulgence. As the heir to the throne of Bharatvarsh, he cared little for decorum. His mother, Sugandha, had raised him to be a carefree spirit, unaware of the great history of his kingdom and the heroic tales of Vikramaditya. Instead, Mahendra found pleasure in the company of his friends, engaging in wild nights of debauchery and drinking.

Once day, Prince Mahendra embarked on a journey towards Kishkindha with his companions Koop and Sanyu. The city of Kishkindha was perched atop a majestic mountain peak, and the path leading up to it was adorned with verdant trees. As they made their way, they were greeted by the soothing sounds of a river flowing down from the mountain top, cascading in beautiful harmony. Just as the evening was setting in, a light drizzle descended from the sky, adding to the charm of their journey. As they rode towards Kishkindha Bhawan on their horses, their eyes fell upon a girl, who was as beautiful as nature itself. Her rosy cheeks and swaying waist mesmerized them. The sight of her belly visible through her black saree left them entranced. The girl was running in the drizzle, clutching a book, on her way to her destination. Mahendra and his companions couldn't resist teasing her, following her closely.

Koop said, "Bulbul! Come on top of my horse." Sanyu joined in, laughing, and saying, "Come to me. I will make you sit on my thighs. You will have a lot of fun." Mahendra kept laughing after hearing all this.

In the meantime, Sanyu dismounted from his horse and tried to forcefully lift the young woman. But she turned out to be courageous. She injured him with a small hidden sword kept near her waist. Fearlessly, she said, "Be careful! You live in the reign of Vikramaditya and do not know how to respect women. If I inform him about this despicable act of yours, all three of you will be severely punished." Then, looking at Mahendra, she said, "Prince! You should die of shame. I doubt whether he is your father or not. Your father is like Shri Ram and, on the contrary, you are like the evil Ravan."

Koop began to attack the woman with his sword, but Mahendra stopped him. The woman left from there. After she was gone, Koop said, "Prince, let's kill her and throw her in this flowing river. She is an evil one who called you Ravan."

Mahendra replied, "She will find out today what Ravan can do".

They pursued the elusive maiden whose name was Avantika all the way to the magnificent city of Kishkindha. It didn't take long for them to uncover her dwelling place. Avantika, a young woman who had tragically lost her parents the previous year, was now living alone and tirelessly studying to pass the entrance exam for Taxila. Her admiration for the great Vikramaditya knew no bounds, and she drew strength from his remarkable journey - from humble beginnings to the revered position of King. Her unwavering determination was known throughout the city, and she fearlessly lived alone in her abode.

Mahendra and his comrades arrived at Kishkindha Bhavan, the echoes of "Ravan" still ringing in his ears, stoking the flames of his thirst for revenge. As night fell, they drank, and the alcohol stirred up Koop's dark thoughts. "Prince," he slurred, "that woman must be punished for her crime." Sanyu nodded in agreement. "She must learn that Mahendra is the future ruler of Bharatvarsh. It's time for her to forget about Vikramaditya."

Mahendra, already intoxicated, fumed, "I don't understand what's so special about that Vikramaditya. He married my mother Sugandha but didn't love her. And then he slept with another woman after their marriage! How can he be an ideal? He never loved his own son because of that woman!"

Sanyu interjected, "Just be patient, Mahendra. You will soon sit on the throne as new king of Bharatvarsh."

Koop added, "But Prince, you need to toughen up. You can't let a mere girl disrespect you like this."

Mahendra's desire for revenge burned hotter with each passing moment, and Lust had overtaken them all. They decided to visit the girl's home and teach her a lesson.

Intoxicated with alcohol and consumed by a thirst for revenge, the three men made a decision to barge into the young woman's home. Avantika, lost in her studies by the light of a lamp in the dead of night, had no idea of their impending arrival. Suddenly, they caught her off guard, overpowering her with ease. Koop swiftly covered her mouth with a cloth, leaving Avantika in a state of shock and unable to cry for help. Trembling with fear, they stripped her naked and completely pinned her down. Tears of blood streamed down Avantika's face as Mahendra savagely raped her, his cohorts cheering him on. As they left, Sanyu and Koop also inflicted their own vicious assaults upon her. They tossed some gold coins at her before they all fled into the night.

After some time, Avantika regained consciousness. She was feeling thirsty, but she was unable to stand up. The light of the lamp had gone out. She pulled her body to the kitchen. She was unable to get up and drink water. She started quenching her thirst by licking the water that had fallen down. She started crying bitterly. She hated herself. She kept crying until morning. She could not understand why this had happened to her. Now she started cursing God too. Her soul was more broken than the body. She wrote a letter to Rajan Vikramaditya while crying, describing the incident that happened to her and demanded justice.

In just a few days, this letter reached Vikramaditya. When Vikramaditya read this letter, he was overcome with a deep sense of distress. His own son had committed a despicable act towards a young woman - an act that he found to be truly unimaginable Now, due to the comparison with Shri Ram, he has begun to worry more about his reputation. He did not want his prestige to be tarnished in any case. After reading the letter, he immediately burned it so that no one would come to know about the incident.

As per the orders of Kaliyuga, Attachment began to dominate over Vikramaditya, but this attachment was not for his son, but for his own prestige.

Vikramaditya wrote a letter to Avantika inviting her to meet him at a deserted area outside the city of Kishkindha. Vikramaditya went to meet her without telling anyone.

Avantika hoped for justice from King Vikramaditya. She came out of the city with his letter to meet him.

It was night and everything began to become hazy. Avantika met King Vikramaditya while crying. She had never thought that she would meet the person whom she had idealized since childhood in such a pitiful state. She told King Vikramaditya about her suffering and asked him to punish Mahendra.

Avantika said crying, "I feel disgusted with myself. I hate my own body. Those people committed the crime, but I am suffering from the shame of their crime. I have forgotten my dreams. I wanted to be a part of your administration. But now, I have lost everything. I want to regain my lost respect. It will only be possible when Prince Mahendra and his companions receive harsh punishment. Only then can my soul find peace and I can forget these wounds on my body."

Then wiping her tears, she said, "You are like Shri Ram for us, but your son is the opposite of you. I could have gone into your justice system, but I do not want your honour to be hurt because of Mahendra. You yourself should take notice of this situation and give harsh punishment to the culprits."

Vikramaditya remained silent as he listened. He kept his gaze down. The allure of prestige had clouded his judgement and he was about to commit a crime that would tarnish even his good deeds. As soon as Avantika quieted down, he placed a bag filled with gold coins in front of her. Avantika was stunned. Seeing this, the memory came flooding back to her of how the three of them had committed a heinous act and then threw gold coins at her. She never expected such behaviour from her ideal Vikramaditya. Her hopes of justice were shattered. She had always considered Vikramaditya as her role model, but today her belief was proven false.

She angrily said, "There is no difference between you and your son. You don't even know how to respect a woman. You have become so blinded by your attachment to your son that you have forgotten your duty as a King. You are not even worthy of being compared to Shri Ram." With tears in her eyes, she took a step back and plunged the sword strapped to her waist into her stomach, committing suicide. Vikramaditya tried to stop her, but he failed. She died in his arms, and he began crying loudly. He never thought that this could happen.

It was now raining heavily in the dark night, and a terrible storm had arrived. Everyone was inside their houses. Vikramaditya burned the letter brought by Avantika and then carried her body outside. His legs trembled as he carried her, and his hands and clothes were red with her blood. He was crying, but he still wasn't thinking about justice for Avantika. He didn't want to compromise his prestige under any case. The people compared him to Shri Ram, and if anyone found out about Mahendra's deeds, then he would lose all his reputation and prestige. Due to this obsession with prestige, he threw Avantika's body into a deep pit.

Vikramaditya returned to the royal palace and secluded himself in his room for many days. He was consumed by guilt for the death of Avantika and his mental state deteriorated day by day.

Vayuvraj went to his chamber and saw his condition, and immediately called a doctor. Even the ministers of the king were disturbed seeing his condition. But Mahendra was pleased to see Vikramaditya in such state, as he knew that very soon, he would become the king. Sugandha was also not upset after seeing Vikramaditya's condition. Medication was given to Vikramaditya, but it had no effect on him. He did not even come out of his chamber; he sat in the dark. At night, he remembered Vaidehi and extended his hands to embrace her and cried.

At this time, if Vaidehi was there, he would have accepted his sin in front of her and stepped down from the throne to make her the ruler of Bharatvarsh. He considered Shri Ram as his ideal, but what he did with Avantika made him fall in his own eyes. One of his deeds put an end to all the good deeds of his entire life. He started hating himself and one day he left the palace and took a water burial in the ocean due to his hatred for himself.

The news of Vikramaditya's disappearance spread throughout the nation. The people were distressed and anxious. Vayuvraj deployed the entire army to search for him. When Muni Sahadri heard this sad news, he too hurried to the palace with great concern. The sudden disappearance of a king like Vikramaditya was a source of sorrow and bewilderment for everyone.

"But everyone failed to find Vikramaditya. After several days, fishermen saw a body floating in the sea in the south. They brought the body ashore, and upon seeing it started screaming " Rajan-Rajan".

Vayuvraj was informed of the news and immediately rushed to the site. Overwhelmed with grief, he wrapped himself around Vikramaditya's body and began to cry. The king's lifeless body was then brought to the palace, where the news of his death had already spread like wildfire. People from all walks of life, young and old alike, had gathered at the palace to pay their respects and mourn the loss of their beloved leader. The sound of their wailing echoed throughout

Bharatvarsh, creating a deafening chorus of grief that had never been heard before.

Despite the outpouring of sorrow, nobody knew why the king had taken his own life. Even Muni Sahadri, who loved Vikramaditya like his own son, could not contain his grief. The memory of their first meeting filled him with heartache as he looked upon Vikramaditya's lifeless face and uttered, "Son, you did not deserve such a death." He wailed uncontrollably, raising his voice to the sky as he declared, "Oh Prabhu! Vikramaditya's life has been a guiding light for the entire human society. He brought Ram Rajya in this Kaliyuga. He cannot have such death. If my thousands of years of penance are true, then he will be reborn and make his death as inspiring as his life."

After performing final rites, Vikramaditya's body was cremated, and his son Mahendra ascended to the throne. Vayuvraj, however, chose a different path. Grief-stricken by the loss of his friend, he abandoned his worldly possessions and became a sage living in the forest.

15. The Rise of Chandrabhan

After demise of Vikramaditya, Mahendra ascended to the throne of Bharatvarsh. He ascended to the throne not because of his merit, but solely because of his lineage as Vikramaditya's son. Sugandha performed his coronation. As soon as he became king, he became engulfed in the greed for power. He was constantly grappled by lust. Because of his misdeeds, he first changed Vikramaditya's judicial system. Now, no one could punish the king. He did not understand the spirit of service towards the people. During Mahendra's reign, instability began to increase. Even army also began to consider rebelling against him.

Chandrabhan took full advantage of this opportunity. He had never imagined that Vikramaditya would move out of his way like this. It was no longer difficult for him to dethrone Mahendra. He began to use more politics in his warfare. Within two years of Mahendra becoming king, Chandrabhan organized a huge army and began his victory campaign from the eastern region. He wanted to make his supporter Nilanka the king of this region. He joined forces with Nilanka and attacked the capital of the eastern region, Atayapur. The king of this place was Ajjtya who responded appropriately to this invasion. However, Chandrabhan was a great warrior, and no soldier of Ajjtya could face him. After a few days, Ajjtya and his capable warriors fled the battlefield out of fear of Chandrabhan. Chandrabhan had achieved his first victory. He went ahead and surrounded the Atayapur palace and sat there with his caravan. Nilanka was surprised by Chandrabhan's decision and said while looking at him - "My king! Why don't we go inside the palace and claim our rights? Ajjtya has fled from the battlefield and accepted his defeat. I want to kill him and claim the throne of Atayapur. After that, with all my strength, I will support you in claiming the throne of Bharatvarsh."

Chandrabhan spoke seriously, "Ajjtya will now seek help from Mahendra, but he is immersed in royal luxury and is weak. He won't be able to help Ajjtya. We will not attack the palace for a week. Every state in Bharatvarsh should know that in front of Chandrabhan, Mahendra is incapable of helping them. No one should think that Mahendra was unable to help Ajjtya due to lack of time. They should know that Mahendra lacked courage, not time."

Nilanka chuckled and said, "Your strategy sounds perfect. After a week, I will eliminate Ajjtya and claim the throne of Atayapur." Then, he turned towards the soldiers and commanded, "Secure all the exits of the palace. Ajjtya must not be allowed to flee."

The letter of assistance from Ajjtya was delivered to the Raj Bhavan of Prasthapur through a messenger. The envoy of Ajjtya read the letter and requested for assistance. The entire assembly became worried upon hearing this letter. General Veerdhvaj proposed an immediate declaration of war against the rebel Chandrabhan in front of King Mahendra.

King Mahendra responded, "General, have you not considered the fact that Chandrabhan is a skilled warrior? Defeating him would require deploying our entire army, and my throne would be at risk. This is not a risk I am willing to take." The entire assembly was stunned by the king's statement.

Minister Swarkar spoke up, saying, "King, this is unacceptable. It is our responsibility to assist Ajjtya in this crisis. He was a close friend of Vikramaditya and always strived towards the dream of Ram Rajya."

Veerdhvaj spoke angrily, "King! if you do not help Ajjtya, soon your throne will be taken away."

Mahendra stood up, seething with anger, and retorted, "Veerdhvaj, stay within your limits. I am the king, and I do not need Ajjtya, who fled the battlefield like a coward. We will make peace with Chandrabhan, which will be more beneficial for us."

Saying this, Mahendra left the court. Meanwhile, Ajjtya waited for the assistance, but no one came, and a week passed. Nilanka spent this week anxiously. The next morning, they were about to launch an attack. Nilanka was eager to attain the throne, and he even shared his enthusiasm with Chandrabhan.

Chandrabhan smiled and said, "Tomorrow you will surely sit on the throne of Atayapur."

Hearing Chandrabhan's assurance, Nilanka felt elated. The army was prepared for the final phase of the war. However, that very night, Chandrabhan sent his message through Vrijbhan, which reached Ajjtya.

Vrijbhan quietly made his way into the palace. Ajjtya knew Vrijbhan for last many years. Upon being informed of Vrijbhan's arrival, Ajjtya agreed to meet him. Vrijbhan informed Ajjtya, "Respected King, tomorrow we plan to attack the palace. It is in your best interest to leave with your family from the southern gate of the palace today itself. My soldiers will escort you to a safe place."

Ajjtya couldn't help but ask, "Are you planning to deceive me?" Vrijbhan replied firmly, "You know me well. I do not deceive, and neither does Chandrabhan believe in such tactics."

Ajjtya still had many questions in his mind and he asked, "But, why is Chandrabhan helping me?" Vrijbhan simply answered, "Only Chandrabhan knows that. You should leave from here tonight. Mahendra will not come to help you."

Saying this, Vrijbhan left from there. Ajjtya had no other option. He trusted Vrijbhan and left the palace with his family. The soldiers of Chandrabhan's army led him to a safe place where Nilanka would't find him.

The next morning, Chandrabhan invaded the palace with Nilanka and took it over without any resistance, but Ajjtya had already left. Nilanka was very disappointed, but Chandrabhan calmed him down. Chandrabhan crowned Nilanka as the new king and thus Chandrabhan succeeded in his conquest campaign in the eastern region.

Meanwhile, disagreements were increasing between King Mahendra, General Veerdhvaj, and the ministers. In thc midst of this, Chandrabhan succeeded in installing his aide Traanj as the ruler in the southern region of Bharatvarsh. He now began to gain full control over the eastern and southern regions. King Mahendra was still immersed in his royal pleasures and was unable to see the danger looming over him.

Chandrabhan began preparations to attack Prasthapur. This war was to fulfill his ambition of ascending to the throne of Bharatvarsh, a dream he had cherished since childhood. He marched towards Prasthapur with a massive army and his aides. His army was composed of horse riders, swordsmen, and archers, who were capable of fighting in any situation. The best warriors, such as Nilanka, Traanj, Kashav, and Yugam, were part of his army.

In a few days, he arrived at the city of Chitrapur near Prasthapur with his massive army and settled his camp there. Chandrabhan only discussed his strategies with Vrijbhan. Upon reaching Chitrapur, he discussed his further strategy with Vrijbhan and sent one of his messengers to the royal palace of Prasthapur.

Chandrabhan's messenger began reading his message in the royal court of Prasthapur. The messenger boldly spoke in royal court of Prasthapur in front of King Mahendra, "Chandrabhan believes in peace, not war. If you accept his proposal, he will end this war. He wishes to negotiate with you. Send General Veerdhvaj and Minister Swarkar for negotiations immediately."

After hearing the message, Mahendra chuckled and glanced at his courtiers and said, "I had already told you that Chandrabhan is greedy." Looking towards Veerdhvaj, he said, "General! Immediately proceed with this matter. Convey to him fear of our military might. Fulfill all his worldly desires and put and immediate end to the war."

At that moment, his minister Swarakar said, "King! Chandrabhan is skilled in politics. You should prepare for war. He will not stop until he attains this throne."

Mahendra replied, "Minister! My decision is final. Veerdhvaj and you will go for the negotiations."

Despite his reluctance, Veerdhvaj prepared for the negotiations. That same night, the venue for the negotiations was decided between Prasthapur and Chitrapur. Vrijbhan and

Chandrabhan attended the negotiations, while King Mahendra was represented by Veerdhvaj and Swarkar.

Everyone arrived at the designated place. Chandrabhan looked at both of them and said, "Thank you for coming to this meeting."

Veerdhvaj said seriously, "What do you want?" Chandrabhan replied, "Peace."

Swarkar said, "That is in your hands. Stop the war." Chandrabhan smiled and said, "You are both wise. My victory in this war is certain."

Veerdhvaj said, "Living in arrogance is not good." Chandrabhan replied, "I know the difference between arrogance and confidence."

Swarkar asked, "Why did you call us?" Chandrabhan replied, "I want you to fulfil your duty."

Veerdhvaj said, "I don't need to learn from you."

Chandrabhan said, "Veerdhvaj! You are the commander of Bharatvarsh, not of Mahendra. Stay away from this internal power struggle. I called you here to explain this to you." Veerdhvaj laughed and said, "You want me to commit treason."

Chandrabhan firmly stated to Veerdhvaj that his loyalty should be towards Bharatvarsh and not towards Mahendra, questioning if he was the commander of the army of Bharatvarsh or Mahendra's slave. He urged Veerdhvaj to stay away from the power struggle and focus on the benefit of the nation. Swarakar accused Chandrabhan of being afraid, but Vrijbhan clarified that their efforts for peace should not be misunderstood as fear and reminded them of their certain defeat.

Chandrabhan emphasized his desire for a nonviolent transfer of power and avoiding the loss of soldiers' lives. Swarakar argued that power has never been transferred peacefully before.

Chandrabhan expressed his love for Bharatvarsh and assured Veerdhvaj of his certainty to ascend the throne. He also shared his vision of freeing the army so that they would always prioritize the nation's security over power struggles. Drawing closer to Veerdhvaj, Chandrabhan emphasized his desire to avoid losing warriors like him and urged for a peaceful transfer of power without any war. He then posed the ultimatum to Veerdhvaj, requiring him to make a decision.

As the conversation concluded, Veerdhvaj and Swarkar departed from the venue, while Vrijbhan and Chandrabhan returned to their caravan.

During the journey, Vrijbhan inquired from Chandrabhan, "Do you think these people will understand?"

To which Chandrabhan responded with confidence, "I trust that they will. Both of them are wise and will take necessary steps for the benefit of the nation."

On the other hand, Veerdhvaj and Swarkar didn't inform Mahendra about this discussion. They pondered over it all night long. The following morning, Chandrabhan advanced with his army. He surrounded the Raj Bhavan of Prasthapur from all sides. Mahendra had no idea about this. Suddenly, Chandrabhan appeared at the royal court with his warriors. He was dressed in a warrior's attire, with a sword hanging by his waist and a shield on his back. He smiled and walked towards the throne. Mahendra also picked up his sword and told Veerdhvaj to detain Chandrabhan immediately.

However, no one listened to Mahendra. Mahendra realized that he had been betrayed. He proceeded alone towards Chandrabhan.

Chandrabhan also drew his sword, and the fight began. In a few strokes, the sword slipped from Mahendra's hands. Chandrabhan pushed him and he fell down.

"Accept defeat. You are the son of Vikramaditya. That's why I'm sparing your life," Chandrabhan stated.

Upon hearing Vikramaditya's name, Mahendra became angry and said - I don't want to owe anything to the name of Vikramaditya. As he said this, he plunged Chandrabhan's sword into his own neck and died. Chandrabhan could do nothing. This battle ended without any bloodshed. Sugandha's life left her body as soon as she saw her son's corpse. Mahendra's ministers and General had already accepted Chandrabhan as their king.

Anasuya has now arrived at the royal court. A few decades ago, she had escaped from this same palace to save her life, but today, due to Chandrabhan's courage, she returned to this palace with honour. She performed Chandrabhan's coronation and Chandrabhan ascended to the throne that he desired. Chandrabhan appointed Vrijbhan as his special advisor, Veerdhvaj as the General, and Swarkar as the Mahamantri. Most people thought that Veerdhvaj and Swarakar were given these positions because they supported Chandrabhan against Mahendra, but they were both capable, and Chandrabhan did not want to lose them.

Now a great challenge was about to unfold for Chandrabhan. Representatives from all the states were now gathered in the royal court.

New powerholders were going to sign a treaty that would determine the future direction of Bharatvarsh. Chandrabhan was seated on the throne. To his left, Vrijbhan and Swarkar were seated, and to his right, Veerdhvaj and his finest warrior were seated.

The first proposal was presented for the treaty. This proposal came from Traanj and it was to declare individuals related to the royal family as of high class. The proposal included giving many privileges to the high class. Everyone welcomed this proposal. Chandrabhan did not entirely agree with it, but he had to accept this proposal for the sake of the royal throne.

Vrijbhan knew that Chandrabhan did not want anyone to be considered high class solely on the basis of their lineage, but he was helpless. Chandrabhan paused for a moment and said, "The proposal is accepted, but the priority in education will not be based on class." The proposal was included in the treaty.

Nilanka brought the second proposal - this proposal was to limit the rights of women. It included reducing their representation in the army and government.

Chandrabhan immediately said, "There is no need for this proposal."

"King, you are mistaken," Nilanka said. "Have you forgotten Vaidehi? Her role was paramount in the destruction of the Sakayu dynasty and the death of your father, Ketubhan."

Following Nilanka' s statement, the crowd began to side with him. Although Chandrabhan held respect for Vaidehi, the people in attendance still viewed him as the son of Ketubhan and did not anticipate him to honor Vikramaditya and Vaidehi.

Chandrabhan pacified the crowd and declared, "Henceforth, women will not be eligible for rulership, but their other rights will remain intact." Despite his desire to uphold Vikramaditya's progressive policies, Chandrabhan knew that his path was fraught with challenges.

Following that, the next proposal was related to revenue. The representatives suggested imposing heavy taxes to increase their treasury, but Chandrabhan did not want to repeat his father's mistakes. He aimed to establish a dynasty that would rule for thousands of years and knew that heavily taxing the people would not be a sustainable approach.

He stood up and addressed the assembly, "I do not want to repeat the mistakes of the past and risk facing rebellions like my father Ketubhan. Levying heavy taxes on our people would not be a sustainable approach. Instead, I propose that the revenue collection be centralized under the Raj Bhawan of Prasthapur and then distributed equitably to all the states under my supervision. This was a very unique proposal for everyone, but everyone accepted Chandrabhan's proposal.

And now the next proposal was made - to shut down Taxila and establish a state-controlled education system. Chandrabhan immediately said, "Taxila is the pride of Bharatvarsh and will remain so. You are afraid of Taxila because the interference of sages in politics. I assure you that it will not happen anymore."

Now Chandrabhan proposed his next idea, "Starting today, we will separate the army from political administration. There should be no violence among the people of Bharatvarsh, be it north, south, east, or west. No state shall maintain an army for war anymore. Only a small number of individuals shall be appointed to maintain the government system and shall not use any lethal weapons." Though this proposal was not unanimously accepted, Chandrabhan cleverly convinced them to do so.

Thus, the treaty of governance was drafted in Bharatvarsh. Chandrabhan endeavored to uphold the principles of Vikramaditya's policies but faced challenges in doing so.

16. The Journey Thereafter

After ascending to the throne, Chandrabhan went to meet Muni Sahadri at the Taxila University. The grandeur of Taxila left him amazed; its massive building was even more stunning than the Prasthapur Palace. Upon passing through the main gate, the king was asked to remove his royal attire and wear ordinary clothing, which he complied with. Chandrabhan, being the son of Ketubhan, made the Acharyas of Taxila University worried about his ascension to the throne. But as soon as Chandrabhan became king, he gave Taxila the right to autonomy. Now, King would not interfere in any of Taxila's affairs. Chandrabhan's humble behaviour assured the Acharyas of Taxila that they could now focus solely on imparting knowledge without any fear.

Chandrabhan visited Muni Sahadri in his chamber. Muni Sahadri was lying on a bed, having already given up food and preparing to leave his body. Chandrabhan greeted him and sat down beside him. Muni Sahadri looked towards Chandrabhan but said nothing. After a while of silence, Chandrabhan spoke - 'I may not be able to become Vikramaditya, but I will strive to fulfill the dream you have seen for Bharatvarsh.'

Muni Sahadri spoke softly - 'No one can become Vikramaditya.'

Chandrabhan replied - 'Because I did not have the support of Muni Sahadri, Vaidehi, Vayuvraj, and a kingdom like Pratipur. But in these tough times, I will lead with the ideas of Vikramaditya.'

Upon hearing the name of Vikramaditya, tears welled up in Muni Sahadri's eyes. He spoke in a soft voice,

"You are caught in the illusion of the royal throne, and because of this, you may fail to make the right decision. However, you are also a disciple of Muni Samved, and Vikramaditya was also his disciple. It was Muni Samved who first suggested that Vikramaditya should become the ruler of Bhartavarsh. That is why I invited him to Pratipur."

Chandrabhan replied, "Vikramaditya was undoubtedly an ideal king, which is why the people started comparing him to Shri Ram".

As Sahadri thought of Vikramaditya, his eyes filled with tears. He regained his composure and turned to Chandrabhan, saying, "You will be the father of a wise, successful, and powerful son who will lead Bharatvarsh to great glory. Your son will accomplish what even the wisest sages will not be able to. But your attachment to him will become the cause of your death, and you will forget the lure of the throne for his sake. Right now, Bharatvarsh needs you, and history will understand you." Sahadri then placed his hand on Chandrabhan's head, giving his blessing.

After hearing Muni Sahadri' s words, Chandrabhan fell silent. He did not fear death, nor was he swayed by attachment to his future son. He felt content with the sage's blessings and after returning from Taxila he set out alone to meet his guru, Muni Samved. Chandrabhan arrived in his regal garments and greeted Muni Samved, who was pleased to see him.

"King, have you received Muni Sahadri's blessings?" inquired Muni Samved.

Chandrabhan smiled and replied, "You all know it."

Muni Samved advised, "King! You should let go of your attachment for the throne and embrace the noble ideals of governance."

Chandrabhan stated, "To me, Vikramaditya is an ideal figure. I will strive to follow his policies."

Upon hearing this, Muni Samved looked at him and replied, "To me, you and Vikramaditya are one and the same. In the Kaliyuga, both of you will be considered as the ideal kings of Bharatvarsh."

Afterward, Muni Samved added, "I will soon depart from this mortal body. This will be our final meeting. "

Chandrabhan felt disturbed but chose to remain silent. Muni Samved then requested him to leave, and Chandrabhan respectfully bid him farewell before returning to the palace.

As he journeyed on, a deep thirst began to gnaw at his throat. He chanced upon a sparkling pond and eagerly quenched his thirst. Suddenly, an arrow whizzed past Chandrabhan's ear and hit a leopard. Chandrabhan turned around and saw the leopard running away. Then, he noticed a young woman approaching from the front, with a bow in her hand and a quiver on her shoulder. She was tall and graceful, her hair reaching down to her waist. Her clothing covered the lower part of her waist and breast. Her face was radiant, and her blue eyes were captivating.

Chandrabhan was taken aback by the young woman's beauty, which reminded him of an apsara. He quickly regained his composure and thanked her for saving his life. The young woman also felt attracted to Chandrabhan, but she was initially filled with anger towards him. However, in the current moment, she forgot her anger and said, "It was not my wish to save your life, but perhaps your death is not yet written." Chandrabhan remained calm and asked, "Did I unknowingly harm you?"

The woman replied, "Who can love someone who becomes king by overthrowing Vikramaditya? How can you hate a king like Vikramaditya?"

Chandrabhan said, "That's not true. King Vikramaditya is an ideal to me. I am also advancing his policies."

The woman laughed and said, "But you have become of high class now." Chandrabhan replied, "That's not true."

Young woman - "If that's not the case, then come with me and explain it to my tribe." Without saying anything, Chandrabhan followed the young woman. He asked for her name, and the woman humbly told him - "Asthika".

After a while, they both reached the tribe. The people of the tribe were melting iron to make useful objects. Everyone recognized Chandrabhan, and they all gathered together, filled with anger towards him. Suddenly, an old woman came up to Chandrabhan, spat at him, and said - "It was he who killed Vikramaditya." Asthika stopped her, and then the chief of the tribe, Nandan, came forward. Seeing Chandrabhan, he said with disdain - "Royal King of high lineage! Why are you here?"

Chandrabhan replied, "I believe that no one is greater or lesser than another."

Yes, at the time of Vikramaditya, it was like that, but not anymore. The people of the city have started to treat us as belonging to a lower class, and this is happening because of you becoming a king.

Immediately, Chandrabhan took a seat beside the furnace and began crafting a sword. Soon, he finished the sword and presented it to Nandan, saying, "I am not separate from you all. I also grew up in the same tribe."

Nandan, maintaining his composure, responded, "But society is changing." Chandrabhan placed his hands on Nandan's shoulders and said, "My friend, everything will be okay in due time. I just need a little more time."

Chandrabhan had a profound impact on Asthika, and they began to meet regularly, eventually leading to their marriage. In due course, the King's wedding to Asthika was solemnized in the traditional manner. Asthika became Chandrabhan's primary confidant and played a crucial role in his decision-making, always keeping the welfare of the people in mind.

During the reign of king Chandrabhan, several decisions were taken for the betterment of people. Three more universities, similar to Taxila, were established, and measures were taken to increase agricultural production without imposing additional taxes on farmers. The citizens were also granted the right to education and healthcare. However, despite these positive changes, discrimination among social classes continued to grow, and Chandrabhan was unable to prevent it. In this way, Bharatvarsh continued to progress under leadership of King Chandrabhan.

www.ingramcontent.com/pod-product-compliance
Lightning Source LLC
LaVergne TN
LVHW091105150826
845673LV00002B/724

* 9 7 8 8 1 1 9 2 5 1 1 0 0 *